CHILDREN

OF THE

SALT ROAD

CHILDREN

OF THE

SALT ROAD

LYDIA FAZIO THEYS

Little
a

Published by Little A, New York

www.apub.com

Amazon, the Amazon logo, and Little A are trademarks of Amazon.com, Inc., or its affiliates.

ISBN-10: 1503943305
ISBN-13: 9781503943308

Cover illustration by Rebecca Mock

Cover design by Tyler Freidenrich and Shasti O'Leary Soudant

Printed in the United States of America

*For John, who absolutely was not the model for Mark
and who has always, always believed in me.*

ONE

CATHERINE

April 1993

Catherine leans her head against the passenger window, grateful that Mark volunteered to drive from the airport. She's not up to these Sicilian roads today. It started almost an hour before their plane landed—the disembodied sense of dread. That part is familiar. But this time there's more, a feeling that this is some kind of last chance for her. Which is ridiculous. It's been only a couple of months, and she's simply getting away, not running away. She just needs to recharge, and that will be easier away from the well-intentioned encouragement of friends and colleagues.

Funny, but most people she knows, seeing her shaken and down, have said something along the lines of "You've faced problems before and bounced back." The irony is, those remarks have made her examine her life and understand that it's not true. She has not bravely surmounted obstacles or dealt with adversity and come back stronger. Somehow, things have always gone her way, and she's never even seen that. Maybe thirty-five is too old to learn how to bounce back.

When Mark hits a pothole, the *aranciata* Catherine is holding flings an orange splash onto her gauzy white blouse. "What a mess."

Catherine dabs with a tissue. "I look like just the kind of person you want staying in your place for five months."

"Sorry." Mark pulls out left to pass a piece of farm machinery sputtering its way down the road.

"No, it's not your fault." They exchange smiles, and Catherine opens her window, feeling herself relax under the spell of the steady, warm wind. Yes. This is why she's here. She looks out over the placid lagoon that hugs the west side of the narrow road. It sparkles and stretches to touch tiny islands in the distance. Weathered wooden signs point out places that until today have been no more than words on a map. Erice, Trapani, Marsala—the musical names make Catherine's heart sing. Even this brief drive has shown her that no amount of reading could have prepared her for the wild beauty of the place. Derelict stone buildings litter the landscape, new next to old, and active farms and vineyards form a haphazard tumble of careless green fields that dare to race down and touch the road's eastern edge. It's a place that has lived so long, it can't be bothered with the usual niceties of planning, building, demolition, and rebuilding. It simply grows on its ancient roots, organically and comfortably, understood by the locals and forever a mystery to anyone else.

"Mark, quick—we're the second turn after this sign."

It's almost too late, but Mark manages to turn onto a long, white sand track sprinkled with mini craters and lined with prickly pear cactus. When a young boy runs in front of the car, Catherine grips Mark's arm. "Look out!"

Mark hits the brakes hard. "What?"

"You didn't see? You almost hit that boy."

"Damn! No. I looked away for a second. Was he—was it really close?"

"Pretty close. He was crossing. Ran somewhere behind those shrubs on the left." They look at each other, acknowledging this reminder of just how delicate life can be.

"That shouldn't have happened." Shaken, Mark begins driving again at half his former speed. He pulls over next to two tiny, elderly Fiats that look as if they might, with a little work, be made to fit together in the trunk of their leased sedan.

Catherine takes in the brown stone house, the matching stone cottage off in the distance, and the large, long wooden building even farther away. "Look at those olive trees. And the water. It's like the land just . . . liquefies . . . and relaxes. You know? Then continues right on out to the horizon."

She turns to Mark, who squeezes her knee, and with a "Can you believe it?" smile, says, "Looks like you picked a winner here."

"I can't wait to sketch this." Catherine gets out of the car and stretches. For a moment the color of the sky prompts a memory of a student squeezing a well-used tube of cerulean blue, laughing as oil paint spritzes from a crack in the wrong end. The image threatens to lead her down a dark path, but she pulls back.

Mark touches her shoulder. "You OK? Was it—"

"I'm fine." She draws away, knowing her smile is too weak to be convincing. "Look, that must be the owner."

A slender, middle-aged woman steps out the front door of the main house, a buff-colored puppy wriggling past her legs. She walks toward them, but the puppy dashes ahead and greets Mark with full-on pawing and tail wagging.

"Hey, guy." Mark crouches down, and the puppy snuffles in his hair.

The woman, wearing jeans and ankle-high work boots, catches up. "Excuse this, please. He is—em—a baby and not too good in behaving. *Basta*, Pippo! Shhh!" This admonition triggers an inexplicable full-body wag, and the woman shrugs, smiling in what appears to be familiar defeat. She holds out her hand. "*Benvenuti*—welcome to Macri and to our farm. I am Giulia Trovato."

With only one skipped beat of her heart, Catherine replies in rusty Italian. As it becomes clear that Giulia understands her, she relaxes, even more so when Giulia continues in English, with a rhythmic Italianate cadence that is beyond charming.

"Let me show you your little house. It's a short walk only." Giulia explains the cottage's quirks as they walk. "And so, not two showers very close together, OK? Unless you like the cold shower."

At the cottage, Giulia unlocks the door. "You maybe don't need to use this key so much. Here, no one comes to find you who shouldn't."

Catherine takes in the cozy sitting room that opens into a beautiful old kitchen. "I love this tile." She runs her fingers across the peacock-blue and yellow glazes. Large windows offer views of the lagoon to the west, the olive trees to the north, and the big barn in an open field to the south. Catherine reaches into her purse for a leather clip and fastens her dark brown hair up and away from her long neck. She can't wait to kick off her shoes.

Walking over to two trunks stacked against the far wall, Mark says, "Thank you, Giulia, for letting us send these ahead. I had no idea we owned so many clothes."

"No trouble at all."

Mark examines the stone fireplace and the dark wood beams of the high ceiling. "Fantastic. This is built to last, huh?"

"Here, we like when things stay. Not like—eh—the disposable everything. But now I have in my oven something almost ready to come out. I will go take care of this now and be back in two minutes to show you the barn."

"Please do. We don't want any fires." As Giulia leaves, Mark joins Catherine, who's looking out the window. "Something interesting?"

"All of it."

When she doesn't elaborate, Mark says, "You thinking about Seth?"

"I'm planning to write to him, Mark. Try to set some of it straight."

"Not that again, Cath. You have to let it go. Isn't that why we came here? Because you wanted to let it go?"

"*You* wanted to let it go. I need to work it out in a way that makes me comfortable."

"How can you even consider telling him where we are?"

"You think he's going to get on a plane and come here? Come on, Mark." Catherine stops, playing their exchange back in her head, astonished at the swift escalation—quiet to loud, calm to angry. She tempers her tone. "I've already sent him our mailing address here."

"It's just not smart. It's asking for trouble. More trouble."

They stare out the window in silence. Catherine is about to speak when Mark points to a figure in the distance. "Looks like Giulia's ready." He turns to Catherine, his expression conciliatory. "Let's not argue about this right now. Here we are—in this beautiful place. And exhausted. Let's just wait a couple of days and then talk it over, OK?"

Relieved to feel the tension defuse, Catherine smiles. "OK."

As they walk to the long, low building, Pippo runs ahead. Catherine's eyes turn inland to the rows and rows of olive trees and the many tones of moody gray-green they provide for the sun to play with. "These are all yours, Giulia?"

"Yes. One hundred hectares—em, about two hundred fifty acres."

"All for olive oil?"

"Most, but also, we sell the olives to eat. My brother—not far from here he has the press for the oil, and also he preserves the olives to sell them. Our family has done this a very long time."

"The trees are magnificent." Catherine envisions them in acrylic and oil, clay and bronze.

"*Grazie.* Some are very old. Maybe three hundred years." They reach the barn. "You must be tired. Travel from New York—always it makes me want to clean up and rest right away."

Catherine puts a hand over the orange stain on her blouse. "You've been to New York, then?"

"Yes. Manhattan and Brooklyn. My cousin lives in Brooklyn, and I have been three times to stay with her. I like it very much there. But my cousin, she says now is not the same as it was." Giulia waves her hand backward over her shoulder, a gesture that could mean last week or last century. "Now, she says it is all yuppie hippies with fancy ideas who live there. In America, things always change, no?" She sighs. "Where do you live in New York?"

Catherine exchanges a quick glance with Mark, who appears to be suppressing an amused smile. "Brooklyn."

"Oh! So nice."

At the barn, Giulia unlocks a broad set of heavy doors. The baleful groan of their massive hinges, whose style matches the shadowy medieval interior, makes Catherine grateful they've arrived before dark. Centered on one of the very long walls of the cavernous space is a bank of filmy windows lighting the midsection like a stage in a darkened theater. Floating dust forms a veil, suspended in midair. It shimmers in the bright light and disappears into dark corners and the even darker lofts overhead, like fog or smoke. Or runaway spirits. In the surreal glow, Mark's windblown blond hair is a translucent and tattered halo.

"This barn is hundreds of years old, but the windows only maybe fifty years."

"This will be perfect for me. And it's just huge!" Catherine eyes the banks of long wooden lablike tables lined up in the windows, the ideal height for art stools.

"If you open the doors on both ends of the barn, you get a big cool breeze from the water."

As Giulia and Mark discuss the windows, Catherine looks toward the west-facing doorway and through it, to the sloping field that washes out to white in the brilliant afternoon sun. She notes a shadow and a movement, and spies a small boy standing in the doorway, backlit by the glare reflected from the water. She waves at him, but he remains still. Catherine turns to Giulia. "Who's the little boy?" When she turns back, he's gone.

"Boy?"

"He was just there, in that doorway. I saw him before. When we drove up. I assumed he lives here—or nearby."

Giulia stands next to Catherine and looks toward the door. "I think there are no children even close to here, but maybe. Or maybe he visits—like you!"

As Catherine runs her hand over the smooth wood of the benchtop, Giulia says, "Do you have children? At home?"

"Us? Oh, no. Not yet, anyway. Maybe, though. Maybe someday."

Giulia smiles. "*Sì, sì.* Maybe someday. When you are ready for the new adventure."

The next morning, Catherine wakes up later than planned, but she lets Mark sleep. She could say she's being thoughtful, but the truth is she's happy to put off the unpacking.

Choosing a pair of turquoise-and-lime-green ceramic mugs from a kitchen cabinet, Catherine places them on the dark wood table and arranges two chairs for a view of the sea. She locates the coffee grinder—manual, so nice and quiet—and soon wonderful aromas fill the room. Warming milk, fresh coffee beans, even the smell of propane when she lights the burner—they bring back happy memories of time spent living in a cramped apartment with two other graduate students every bit as much in the thrall of Florence as she was. Coffee brewed and milk heated, she sits at the table, her back to the bedroom door. Being here is thrilling and scary, but not as scary as staying in New York. It's one thing to be out of step in a place you're visiting; it's quite another to become out of step in the place you call home. How a single experience can turn your safest place into the one you need to escape—she'd never appreciated how shattering that could be.

"Hello in there?"

Catherine turns to see Mark, elbows on the table, chin resting on clasped hands, seated beside her. Oh, no. That was supposed to stop here—the little gaps in time, the sickening moment when she realizes she's been gone. "I didn't hear you come in. Lost in thought, I guess." She keeps her voice light.

"I'm still half-asleep myself." Mark gets up and walks across the room. "Let's try out this couch."

They plop down on the worn sofa, all wine-colored brocade and plump pillows. Hitching and stretching, they arrange themselves to be close and cozy.

"This thing could swallow you up." Catherine readjusts a leg. "If we look, we might find the last guests down in there."

They sit in quiet for a long time until Mark speaks. "You know, I think we're some of those 'yuppie hippies in Brew-ka-leen-a' Giulia was complaining about."

"Oh God, I know. Let's stay away from that subject with her, OK?" Catherine gets up, again drawn to the window. The sky is so blue it all but demands they get up and out there to find out why it's so happy. "There's that peculiar boy again. He just—stands there." She waves, but he doesn't seem to notice.

"I hope he's not going to be a pest. Hang around us all the time."

She walks back to the couch and puts on her shoes. "It's odd, Mark, but . . ."

"Yes?"

"Well, it must be because we came so close to—you know—hitting him on the way in. But seeing him gave me a weird feeling. Butterflies in my stomach or something. Something—fidgety." She walks back to the window. "He's gone now."

Mark stands and rests his hands on her shoulders and his chin on top of her head. "Hey, with any luck he's visiting someone nearby, and you'll never see him again. Anyway, once he catches on to who we are . . ."

"Who we are?"

"Yeah. A pair of yuppie hippie types from Brooklyn, responsible for the decline and fall of the entire borough. I mean, why would he want to hang around us?"

TWO

SETH

August 23, 1992

Dear Notebook,

I was going to write "Dear Diary" but I felt like a 12 yr old girl with a pink gel pen. I don't exactly know how to feel about this. About you. I mean, it was nice of Dr Whitmore to give me a fancy leather diary. He called it a "graduation" present now that I'm going from once a week appointments to once a month. But the truth is he actually believes that writing about yourself every day is a helpful thing. I guess if you're a shrink you really buy into the whole idea of examining every thought and emotion. Which I don't think I'm all that great at.

It feels pretty okay to be enrolled in school again. My new apartment is kind of a pit, but it's close to CCNY so I'm cool with it. The whole place is brown. And chipped. It's a look, I guess. I said apartment but really it's a room with some kitchen stuff stuck off in one back corner and a bathroom with one of those funky old tubs in the other. Which at least matches the rest of the decor since it's kind of brown and definitely chipped. The refrigerator, though. That thing is old and the only brown is on the inside. It doesn't wash off and I don't even want to know.

I'm supposed to write about how I feel, so— yeah—I still feel down. I'm not sure that's ever gonna change. I've been in therapy nearly 6 months and Dr Whitmore seems to think I don't need to see him so much anymore. I guess he figures pretty soon I'll be all fixed up, but I don't know. You don't just forget something that big and move on. At least not me.

If I'm honest about it, I'm scared right now. I have no friends at CCNY. My friends from RISD—some of them have called me but I won't ever be part of that group again so why pretend and make them pretend? Maybe when we all graduate I'll take the train up to Rhode Island and see them. But I'll worry about that in a couple of years. Same with my old friends here. Everyone's gone their own way pretty much. I'm not part of my old neighborhood anymore, especially after what happened. So I'm starting all over and there's nobody home but me.

THREE

CATHERINE

The lounge chairs Giulia has set up are large, cushioned, and colorful, and this rest is a welcome luxury after today's massive unpack-and-put-away session. Catherine raises one leg, splays her toes, and frames an offshore island in one of the spaces between them.

"Do you suppose the weather is always like this?" Sun-drunk, jet-lagged, and happy, Catherine turns to Mark.

"Mmm." He doesn't bother opening his eyes. "I sure hope so. Hey, didn't Giulia say she and her mother would be here at four?"

Catherine stretches her arms overhead. "We're in Italy, Mark. It's been four o'clock since a little after three, and it will continue to be four o'clock until at least five thirty. But wake up. Here they come."

Pippo arrives first and sets to work on a toe bath for Mark. A smiling Giulia is close behind, holding a silver tray with espresso for four. "I'm sorry about Pippo. He will be adopted later this week, but we must keep him here until then."

"He's sweet." Catherine stands to help Giulia with the tray just as a gray-haired woman, not five feet tall, her chunky, tubular body clothed entirely in black, joins the group.

"This is my mother. You know she lives with me, yes? And she asks you to call her 'Assunta,' nothing more formal, please." Giulia grabs on to Assunta's outstretched arms and slows the older woman's descent-and-drop into the low chair. Assunta says something in a language that resembles Italian—but isn't—as she twists and slides her way toward the backrest.

Giulia sighs. "*Mamma* can speak pretty good Italian and English. But when she feels shy, she speaks the *sicilianu*."

"*Buon pomeriggio*, Assunta." Catherine hopes "Good afternoon" is the right greeting at this time of day. "Would you like a more comfortable chair?"

Mark begins to rise. "If someone tells me where . . ."

Assunta shakes her head and speaks a few quick words.

"*Mamma* says she is good now with this chair."

As if to prove the point, Assunta folds her hands in the slight indentation that marks the meeting of ample bosom and ample abdomen.

"You have a magical place here." Catherine accepts a tiny cup of coffee from Giulia. "We're very grateful you rented it to us."

Assunta smiles and nods as Giulia pours coffee. "*Mamma* and I do not see so many people here who speak English. But after some little time to listen and become accustomed with the ear, *Mamma*'s English will be much better again. Mine too, I hope!"

Assunta takes a deep breath and leans forward, dealing her words like cards from a deck. "What do you plan to do here?"

"Well, I think you know I'm an artist. I plan to work in the barn, mostly drawing and sculpting. And I want to learn more about casting bronze statues. There's an expert who lives in Firenze. I know him from years ago when I was in school there."

"This is what you do at home?"

"Yes. I teach art at City College of New York, but I also paint and sculpt."

"And you, Mark?" Assunta's voice is more confident now.

"I'm an architect. A junior partner at a small architectural firm."

A quick flurry of dialect passes back and forth between Assunta and Giulia. Both women smile and nod. "Architectural *firm*," says Giulia. "This is a funny expression to translate."

Mark explains that he is here to learn about the developing *agriturismo* movement. "Are either of you familiar with it?"

"Yes. *Mamma* and I read about the new laws. I think this is the plan for small farms here to have visitors who come for their holidays? Like you and Catherine come here."

"Exactly. I'll be meeting with landowners all over Italy who want to welcome tourists as guests on their farms. They may need to make some changes to their buildings, or even add new ones, to accommodate their guests."

"Such a good chance for people to see the real Italy." Giulia sweeps one arm from horizon to horizon. "So many people—they know the Coliseum, the Blue Grotto. But they do not know the beauty of the true countryside. Or about how deep is our history here. Even if you must dig a little harder than in some, eh . . ." She wrinkles her nose. ". . . big museum with signs and—eh . . ." She taps her ears. ". . . speakers for your head."

Mark and Catherine share quick, amused smiles as he reaches for a cookie. "I'm looking forward to driving around, meeting people who agree with you."

Assunta crosses herself, and Giulia laughs. "*Mamma* does not approve of driving. She thinks people should take only the train for the long journeys because drivers here are too reckless."

"I'll use the train when I can, so Catherine isn't without a car if I'm gone very long."

"No-no-no! You drive your big car. We have two. And only one who drives—me. Catherine, you can use the other. You buy the petrol only and go."

Assunta crosses herself again.

Catherine turns to Giulia. "I couldn't—"

"I insist." Giulia brushes her palms together. "It is a decision."

"Thank you. That's very generous. I feel at home here already, thanks to your graciousness, Giulia."

"*Buonissima!* It is not easy to compete with an exciting home like New York."

Catherine's smile fades and Giulia says, "I said something to make you sad."

Mark gets up and stands behind Catherine with his hands on her shoulders. She reaches up and places her hands over his. "It's nothing."

"Sometimes things happen and you need to get away." Mark massages Catherine's shoulders. "For a break. A change of scene."

"Yes." Giulia nods. "A change of scene. Maybe sometimes a fresh start. It's good. Good for everybody."

FOUR

SETH

August 26, 1992

Dear Notebook,

I registered for classes today. I waited pretty late, but I got the ones I want. Well, they make some exceptions for transfer students so that didn't hurt. It's really weird not being nagged about anything like registering on time or paying my bills. My mother always kept better track of what I needed to be doing than I ever did. I guess I'm free to screw up now. Ha ha.

Part of me wants classes starting but another part wants to get out of here. I'm not sure where I'd go though since all the memories would come right along with me. And the guilt.

A few months ago, I decided to read the paper every day. I figure I might as well know what's going on out in the world since nothing goes on in my world. Or what's left of it. But it's one bad thing after the other and really depressing. Some horrible stuff goes on. Last month there were 3 big plane crashes. 70 people got killed in one. The other 2—and this is really weird—they were on the same day. 221 people—bam—gone. In China and Nepal. I guess I'm not the only one whose life suddenly went to shit. It's supposed to be that misery loves company, but reading about all that doesn't make me feel better. It makes me feel like it's probably gonna happen again. There was another one. A big flight and everybody got out before the plane went on fire. Yeah, 292 people escaped a fire. And then there was a hurricane. That thing killed 39 people and destroyed 25,000 houses. I can't even imagine it.

I can't stop wondering why I am still even alive. Why I get to sign up for classes and Amy doesn't. She would have been a freshman right now. She never even found out what schools she got into. Dr Whitmore says I feel "understandable" guilt about surviving when she didn't. But, you know, dear Notebook, it's simpler than that. I just feel like shit.

One of the meds he has me taking now makes me really dizzy. Right out of the blue the world starts spinning. Sometimes I wonder if I could just spin apart. I wish I would. Not really. I really don't know what I wish. I more or less stopped wishing a while ago.

FIVE

MARK

Mark walks up to the low, modern office building with a touch of apprehension. This place, which his firm has arranged as his local base of operations for the next five months, is more than a little different from what he's used to in New York. He pulls open one of the heavy glass doors, and the first thing he notices is the aroma of strong coffee and the echoing sound of men, out of sight, talking and laughing. He approaches the receptionist's desk.

"*Buongiorno.* I'm—" He catches himself. "*Sono* Mark Lindquist." Catherine warned him this day would come if he didn't learn Italian. And he didn't. And now he feels every bit as much the ugly American as she'd told him he would.

"*Signor* Lindquist! We've been expecting you." The receptionist's English is quite good, making Mark feel like a simpleton as well. "Welcome. I am Paola. And please—a moment, while I tell *al Signor* Di Mauro that you are here."

Paola picks up the phone, and Mark looks around the reception area, admiring the clean lines of the furniture. He turns at the sound of leather soles snapping across the terrazzo floor.

"*Benvenuto!* I'm Edoardo. We have spoken on the phone." They shake hands and Mark follows Edoardo back into a comfortable conference room. It isn't long before two other men, Giuseppe and Luca, join them.

"Did you have trouble finding us?" Edoardo offers Mark an espresso, then sits at the table.

"None at all. It took about forty-five minutes. I was lucky, though. No traffic."

"You are not saying here in Palermo?"

"No. I'm down the coast—in Macri."

Edoardo's face changes. Mark isn't certain what he sees there. Surprise, for sure, but it's mixed with something else. He watches Edoardo neutralize his expression before speaking. "Macri! Ah, yes. That is a little bit of a drive. But you will be on the road all around Italy, yes? So you won't be there very much?"

"That's right." Pushing aside a flicker of concern for what that remark might mean, Mark decides to ignore it for now and sketches in his plans for the next few weeks.

"Excellent. We are here when you need us or our facilities. Come. You can see what is available."

As they leave the room, Luca and Giuseppe exchange a brief bit of Italian, but the only thing Mark can make out is "Macri." Is he imagining that they look puzzled as well? "Edoardo, are they talking about Macri?"

Edoardo gives the two men a sharp glance. "I'm sorry. Yes, they were talking about the best road to take there."

"Are you sure that's all? There isn't something I should know? Something about Macri or—"

"No, no. You know—the road, the drive—this is always the Italian preoccupation."

◆ ◆ ◆

Marsala, not twenty kilometers along the seaside road from Giulia's farm, is a vibrant city—ancient, artsy, and comfortable in its own skin. Its multicultural history, more than two thousand years' worth, gives it an air of having seen it all and kept only the best. Sitting across from Catherine at an outdoor table near the piazza, Mark notes the way the early-evening light plays on the pale-yellow fronts of nearby buildings, making them appear warm and sun-soaked even now. His architect's eyes fill with inspiration: the wrought iron balconies, the flower boxes brimming with luscious blooms, and the incredible variety of doors— from tiny and narrow to huge and imposing.

A slender young woman in a crisp white blouse and black slacks brings their orders of Pasta Norma, local red wine, and huge salads topped with fresh basil leaves the size of a child's hand.

Mark places his napkin in his lap. Catherine folds her hands under her chin, elbows on the table. "This whole place—it makes me so happy, I feel like proposing to you."

"Again? It took the first time, you know." He tucks into his pasta. "And seems to have worked out for the last ten years."

"Pity. I mean that I can't do it again."

Mark leans in toward Catherine, and lowering his voice, assumes what he thinks passes for an aristocratic British accent. "However, my dear, we *could* carry on quite indecently." He covers her hand with his and wiggles his eyebrows up and down in a salacious dance. "When we get back to the cottage, of course."

"Maaaay-beee," says Catherine, sipping her wine. "Talk to me again after the pasta."

He sighs. "Looking at this table, I can't honestly fault your priorities."

They both laugh. He raises his hand a discreet distance, and when the waitress looks, he points to the empty wine carafe. She nods and disappears into the restaurant.

Catherine looks down the narrow little street where a blue-gray sliver of sea is still visible in the fading light. "Next stop across that water is Tunisia."

"A ferry goes there, you know. From Palermo. We could take it."

They spend dinner discussing all the places, near and far, they'd like to go. Anything feels possible tonight. When they leave their table, they walk, holding hands like schoolkids, toward the faint sound of music in the piazza. Rounding the corner, they enter the large, busy square, and the sound resolves into the voices of costumed children singing and dancing. At the far end of the piazza is a temporary stage, the strong, tall front of the eight-hundred-year-old church, Chiesa Madre, to its left. Parents and family crowd around.

Mark puts his arm around Catherine's shoulders as she explains that the music is traditional to this area. "Their teacher—I think that's their teacher—just invited the kids' parents onstage to dance with them."

Mothers and fathers climb the steps to the stage—laughing, smiling, and commenting when the music begins—and they sing and dance along with the children. Mark can sense Catherine becoming emotional as she watches the crowd, many of whom sing along softly.

"I've never seen anything like this, Mark. This is their tradition in a way I can't even imagine. And it's almost as if we're part of it."

He does feel part of it, unsure of why it touches him as it does—these strangers who speak a language he can't understand, carrying on a tradition he's never seen. But it touches Catherine, and that's enough for him.

By the time the performance ends, it's close to dark. Street lamps light the city to a warm copper as Mark and Catherine walk to their car, arms around each other's waists. Mark wonders if Catherine is so quiet because she too is marveling at whatever it is that has brought them here, together, to this perfect place with the perfect partner on this perfect night.

◆ ◆ ◆

Lying on a narrow strip of sand, Catherine and Mark form a T, her head cushioned by a folded towel on Mark's stomach.

"How's the headache?" Mark adjusts his sunglasses and brushes sand from his forehead.

"Never let me have that much wine again." Catherine sits up and Mark follows. The calm of the water still surprises him. At most, the lagoon produces a steady train of low ripples in acknowledgment of the never-ending African winds. He looks along the shore where gentle sandy curves form small beach areas. An unusual sight catches his eye, and he squints to see it more clearly.

"Cath? Look. There." He points. "What do you see?"

Catherine looks with and without her sunglasses. "You mean that guy? Or woman, maybe. Way down there?"

"Yeah. Walking on the water. Not that they really can be."

"Well, there aren't enough of us for this to be a collective hallucination, so—"

"But look." Mark points again, as if to be sure Catherine is looking at the right place. "He's definitely on foot, but he's out in the middle of the water."

"It is really weird. But he's so far away. Maybe if we were closer . . ."

"I suppose. And I suppose everything has some boring explanation in the end. Although this one sure beats me right now."

Back at the cottage, Mark parks next to the red Fiat. It's hours before sunset, but the sky has already changed, as if the bright part of the day has been packed up and put away until tomorrow.

"That car." Mark shakes his head. "You should get the brakes checked, anyway. At least."

"You worry way too much." Catherine gathers up their blankets and towels. "Get that picnic basket, would you?"

Catherine may think he worries too much, but he's pretty sure he worries just right and is about to say so when he feels something at his heels. It's Pippo. Mark crouches to pet the puppy, who jumps into the car and with complete lack of finesse jams his head into the picnic basket. When Giulia arrives, she scoops Pippo up.

"Your delivery came today. Everything is in the barn as you asked."

"I hope it wasn't too much trouble." Mark scratches Pippo's ears.

"None at all. Anything I can do for you, please ask."

"Well, maybe you can answer a question. We saw someone—" He pauses. "Who was—well, looked like he was—walking on the water. To the south of your beach here."

Giulia laughs. "You are not the first to be confused by this. That is where you find the evaporating pools for the salt production. And the pools—they are very big and square with narrow stone—eh—I am not sure what you call this—maybe border?—around them. People walk along them sometimes, and from far away, it looks like magic."

"Ah. I had no idea."

"Oh, you must take some time and learn about this. Producing the salt from the sea is an ancient art for us. *Lo Stagnone*—our lagoon—has given back much salt, going back almost three thousand years."

"Three thousand. The Phoenicians?"

"Yes. To know truly our little piece of Sicily, you must go to our salt museum. It is not so big, but you will learn about how the salt is captured, and you will see the beauty of the windmills. This sea salt—it is very much a part of us here."

"Mark?" Catherine is perhaps twenty feet behind him, hugging herself, shoulders hunched.

He joins her. "What's up, Cath? You cold?"

"You just missed him. It was that boy again."

"You're shaking. I hope you're not getting sick."

"I wanted to ask Giulia about him, but she's left. That doesn't seem like her."

Mark turns to see Giulia halfway back to the house, throwing a stick for Pippo and bending down, clapping her hands when he runs after it. "She must have run after Pippo." But really, she's so polite. Leaving like that—it does seem odd.

SIX

Seth

September 17, 1992

Dear Notebook,

Yesterday was my best day in a long time. I still feel like crap but for a couple of hours anyway, it wasn't as bad. My classes are all okay but Art 320 is great. The whole class is juniors and seniors and we have a lot of freedom. Professor Altimari is really something and she pays attention to everybody in there. It feels like we really matter. Like our work is something serious. It's not that my classes at RISD weren't really good. They were. But this is something different somehow.

When I get going in there, a lot of stuff comes into my mind that I wish wouldn't. Not that I ever go very long without thinking about it but painting, drawing—it taps down into the worst of it. Like it should, I guess. And yeah, it feels good to let some of it out but still—it's not gone. In the movies some sweaty artist paints this crazed mad-looking canvas full of stuff and he exorcises his demons. Not me, though.

I was working on this one painting from a model who looked a lot like Amy and when I was done I could see the painting really was Amy and it was all twisted and confused. And then the whole night came back to me right there in class, like it was all happening again. I felt trapped. Like I might lose it in front of the whole class before I could get to the door. But I think I got out before anyone noticed anything. That painting, though—I'm too lazy to explain it, Notebook. You'll have to look at it yourself.

An earthquake killed 116 people in Nicaragua. And there's a horrible flood in Pakistan going on right now. No one really knows but they think maybe 2000 people could be dead there and whole villages are under water. All from rain. It's not even like fire. I mean, fire isn't supposed to happen but rain is. Nothing is safe.

I'm still in a fog half the time. Some of the kids from class went out together but I begged off. Not ready. Not yet. Don't tell anyone, Notebook, but I'm not sure I'll ever be or that I even care. I think Dr W was right. I shouldn't have stopped working all those months. I should have made myself at least sketch or something. Because now that I started again, I realize how much I missed it.

SEVEN

CATHERINE

As soon as Mark's car was out of sight this morning, Catherine had missed him. At the same time, she'd welcomed a full week of no one to play tourist with, meaning an opportunity for some serious work. Now, Catherine drags open the large creaking doors on one end of the barn, or as she thinks of it, her studio. Opening the doors is like drawing back the curtain to reveal a show—a waltz of slowly swirling dust eddies caught unawares by the silent entering sunlight. Groans and echoes of groans chorus from the lofts as the ancient boards expand and contract throughout the day. And the brightly illuminated central area lives in its own window-lit spotlight, its borders blending through dusty dimness into the complete darkness of the barn's corners, edges, lofts, and roof. Mark considers it a little too creepy for comfort. He said opening the doors reminded him of that scene from *Poltergeist* where the kids' bedroom door opens to reveal toys swirling around. But Catherine finds herself drawn to the place. She can't wait to get to work.

Several days before, she'd devoted an entire day to unpacking the crates and boxes of art materials and making the space her own. Most of the setup was mechanical but satisfying: placing sketch pads, charcoals, pencils, erasers, paint, canvases, materials for armatures—all the tools of her trade—in just the right places for easy access while leaving the best spots free and clear for working.

Unpacking several boxes of paintbrushes, she'd sorted them by size and placed them bristles up into white ceramic jars. She'd done the identical thing this past September, setting up for a new semester of Art 320 students. That was always one of her favorite studio classes. The students were experienced and serious, and each class held at least one or two very talented kids. It was all potential then, and the prospect of what her students might create was always exciting. She looked forward to helping them progress with new skills and techniques as they looked at painting in new ways or learned to draw from live models. Some semesters played out to be more satisfying than others, of course, but this last semester—how did it get so bad? She should have seen it coming sooner. It had been her job to stop it before things went completely off the rails. Even with a sabbatical here and an entire semester's break from teaching, she isn't sure she will ever again feel confident of her ability to read students or to handle tricky situations. And how will she teach, why should she be given the responsibility of a class, without those two basic skills?

Today, work has been going well, and she cleans up, planning to take Giulia's Fiat out for the first time. She is considering where to go when an uneasy feeling comes over her, the feeling that someone is watching. She quashes the urge to back up and press flat against the nearest wall, and yet her overwhelming sense is not of threat but of a palpable curiosity. With a mix of reluctance and anticipation, she turns, and there, no more than thirty feet away, is the boy. She can see he's young—four, perhaps five—and wears sandals and brown shorts. His tan-and-red-striped T-shirt is not new, and the fit is snug. His eyes are large, his expression serious, his cheeks lush and round—the face of a near baby with curly brown hair. She thinks of an illustration from a children's book, a Little Golden Book from the 1950s she remembers fondly.

For reasons she takes no time to analyze, Catherine feels an instant connection to the boy, and she smiles, but he turns and runs. Catherine pursues him through the long, dark expanse of the barn and out into the wide-open field. He's gone. She stops. She turns, squinting in the brightness, looking in every direction. As impossible as it seems, because she can't see a single hiding spot even remotely close enough, the child is nowhere in sight.

Behind the wheel of the boxy red Fiat, Catherine is a child playing hooky. She hopes Giulia won't mind that she removed the two bunches of herbs that were hanging from the rearview mirror. Were they decorative? Some kind of local air freshener? Well, at least in the backseat they can freshen the air without blocking her view. She should be working now, as she did yesterday and the day before, and she'd tried. But she'd squandered the morning flitting without focus from one thing to another. So now she's on the road to the Archaeological Museum in Marsala. Yes, she should have waited for Mark, but this spontaneous visit is for inspiration. They'll go again together when he gets back.

She'd hoped to see the boy again, but he hasn't returned, at least not that she'd seen. Or felt. That awful sense of being watched—she's had it before, but somehow this has been different, intense and, for want of a better word, visceral. And demanding. Well, it's probably nothing. The barn, as much as she loves it, is a little eerie, and the brain can be quite the trickster.

Parking in a large lot, empty save for two other cars, she heads off along the pink-brick sidewalk that hugs the museum's long cream-colored front. Across the road to her left, the Mediterranean, gray and choppy compared to the lagoon, extends to the horizon, the sun perched above it, resting up for its spectacular exit later on. A brisk wind off the sea blows Catherine's skirt and hair to one side, then drops them without warning, as if needing a breath, before beginning again. Once inside the door, faced with the shock of sudden stillness and quiet, she decides to start with the room on the right since the only other visitor, a middle-aged man with a notebook, has gone left. A full-size Punic ship, reconstructed into an imposing display, greets her when she turns the corner. Typewritten cards report that this ship had been in the battle ending the First Punic War more than two thousand years ago, sunk on what might have been its maiden voyage. Archaeologists have used all available pieces of the ship, filling in with a skeleton of curved wire and wood. The result is so light and airy, so full of life, that it wouldn't surprise her if the ship burst from the room, flying across the road to the sea, to seek a chance to sail another day.

Hundreds of amphorae, jugs that once held oils and spices, line the back and sides of the room. The entire display fills Catherine with a palpable sense of the people who'd sailed this ship. She can almost see and hear—even smell—the oarsmen as they labored, young men powered by adrenaline and fear. She sits in a corner on the floor, studying the ship until a guard approaches, asking with concern if she's all right. Perhaps *la signora* would like to visit the archaeological park outside since it will soon close? The realization that she has been here for hours shocks Catherine to her feet. She takes the map the guard offers and exits through the double glass doors at the back of the building.

The ruins comprise a vast area of semi-maintained paths through a patchy confusion of greenery and wildflowers. Pale-lavender moths scatter in ghostly clouds as she passes by. Glanced by low shafts of sunlight, bits and pieces of ancient structures poke through in surprising places. Worn-away informational signs and broken floodlights testify to a past formality long gone. Ancient baths, houses, shops, a Roman road, some mosaics—all are visible, nestling into the earth, reaching out here and there to greet the present.

Catherine sees from the map that the archaeological park carves a broad rectangle deep into Marsala with walls, buildings, and fences dividing it from the modern-day city. But who chose the boundary between past and present? She pictures every home, church, and shop sitting on top of more of this, to be discovered only when someone digs a pool or a foundation for a new building. So many artists and scientists must want to know what's there, but you can't very well ask people to let their homes be destroyed to bring more of the past into the present.

Spotting a side exit, Catherine passes through a rusted gate. Almost immediately on the other side sits a small church—a plain, whitewashed box with hazel wooden doors open and inviting. Inside, she finds a modest altar, some pews, and a few statues. Two older men sit toward the back on folding wooden chairs. Conscious of the clipped echo of her every step, she walks to a small grating covering an opening in the stone floor and looks down to the darkness below. One of the men, dressed in a beige linen suit, approaches. Speaking slow, clear Italian, he asks if she would like to see the lower level of the church. "Most interesting," he says.

Catherine follows him down an ancient and crude stone stairway; she bends low to avoid the uneven surface overhead. At the bottom, she looks up at the only source of meager light, the grating in the floor above them.

"This is very special. You will see. And someone like you—you will appreciate it. This, I know."

"Someone like me?"

"I can see you feel that there is something for you here. Most simply pass us by. They never know."

Using a small key, he turns a switch on the wall, and the lights come on with a resonant snap. In front of her, frescoes cover one wall of the large cavelike room. She learns from the gentleman—his speech always clear, patient, and elegantly serious—that the paintings are Roman. A statue of Saint John the Baptist occupies a niche in another wall, a location it first assumed in the 1400s. And in the floor, directly under the grating above, is a deep hole, much like a well. Water trickles from the wall under the statue of Saint John—sweet water, the man says—and meets the seawater inside the hole. This, he explains, is the tomb of the Cumaean sibyl, the very oracle Aeneas visited before his descent into the underworld. The early Christians, believing this sibyl had foretold the birth of Christ, honored this spot and used the sacred waters for baptisms.

He continues speaking, but Catherine only half listens. She feels she's looking at a slice of a layer cake—a cake of mythology and history. No, she is *in* the layer cake. And as she looks up through the floor to the present-day church above, her mind rises through the roof. She wonders what future layers will look like, what her part in this structure could possibly be. And she wonders why she feels so comfortable here, in this layer, where the present is still far in the future.

Catherine hums to herself as she begins what she hopes will be another in a string of productive workdays. Once-empty tabletops now hold armatures in various stages of completion. Paint has spilled. Pencils and charcoals no longer sport sharp tips. This is the way it should be. It even smells like an art studio now.

Drawing the sibyl's cave, Catherine stops humming as the sense of being watched pours over her. But it's not unpleasant this time, and she wills her shoulders to relax, arranging her face into what she hopes is a benevolent and welcoming smile. Without haste or sound, she rotates her stool, and behind her, not ten feet away, stands the boy, offering for the first time something more than a stolen glance. The recognizable sea-salt odor of childhood and the outdoors penetrates even the sharp scent of dried paints and gum erasers.

Like a bird-watcher, Catherine keeps every body movement slow and soft. She smiles at the boy, and to her delight, he stays, but he remains guarded, so Catherine crosses her legs and resumes drawing. As often as she judges prudent, she steals a peek, and each time, he's in the same spot, face expressionless, apparently engrossed in observing her.

"Do you want to sit?"

The boy tenses and backs a few steps away.

"That's OK!" she says. "You're fine where you are."

She returns to sketching, one part of her mind devoted to maintaining slow, even breaths and wondering why he has this effect on her. Catherine's eraser slides to the floor, and she bends to retrieve it. When she comes back up, the boy is gone, vanished in silence—in the blink of an eye. The barn feels empty.

EIGHT

MARK

Mark sits on his hotel bed, feet up, thinking that so far, things have been going better than he could have hoped. He has no experience with being "on the road" or with being in Italy, and both had worried him. He'd expected to be received like a traveling salesman, but everyone has treated him like a cross between welcome guest and doctor on a house call—thanks, no doubt, to the New York office's thorough job in laying a groundwork of trust here. And, of course, his own diligent efforts to identify and learn all about potential clients. All the people he's met with have shown off their properties—their incredible properties—with enthusiasm, and wanted to hear what he had to say. And, at least here, on the outskirts of Milan, lack of Italian has been a non-issue. Every property owner has spoken enough English to carry on a serious conversation, even if sometimes with the help of a dictionary or a friend.

This might as well be another world from Macri. The whole northwestern part of Sicily is incredibly beautiful, and he's been enjoying it there, but here it feels more like the same century he left in New York. His base office in Palermo is a perfect example. The building is modern, the facilities too, but it's out of place in its world. If the architecture were to match the local culture, well, something Art Nouveau might be a better fit, although in some ways, even late nineteenth century feels generous. Which makes that area a great place for a spectacular vacation, but not as much for work purposes. It's a matter of time before Catherine starts to feel the same way, especially given how much she says she loved Florence. Pretty soon, she'll start to miss the sophistication of that kind of life. Let her take her time, clear her mind, and enjoy the simpler life all she can. It will be good for her. By the time she starts feeling restless, he hopes to have some plans in place that she'll find as enticing as he does.

◆ ◆ ◆

Mark checks his watch. Gary, one of the firm's senior partners, had said he was on a tight schedule, flying back to New York tomorrow. Mark's lucky to be able to catch some time with him, but now Mark is wondering if something has gone wrong. He's about to give up and order when Gary approaches the table. Mark stands and the two men shake hands.

"Look at you, huh? I haven't been here that long, Gary, but I'd say that's an Italian silk suit. A little more fashionable than I'm used to seeing you in."

Gary laughs and sits. "When you spend enough time here, you start to notice these things. And I have to admit you feel like a schlub in a standard-issue American suit." He picks up his menu, gives it a quick glance, and closes it. "So, Mark, tell me how it's going."

"Great, really. There are a lot of enthusiastic owners out there desperate for a way to hang on to the family farm."

"We're in this at the perfect time. Handle this right and I think you know—you're looking at senior partner. And, of course, a lot more time coming back here."

Senior partner. The words Mark has been waiting for. "I'll do my best. You can count on it."

"I have no doubt that you will. I'm going to have to run pretty quickly, so—" Gary signals the waiter, and they order. "I'll be back here in about a month, though. Barb is coming with me. For a little vacation. Maybe the four of us can get together—if Catherine's schedule permits."

"I'll look forward to it, Gary. We both will."

"Catherine's—she's doing well?" Gary's good. His voice conveys precisely the right combination of expecting a yes and assured understanding if the answer is no.

"She is, Gary. She is." Mark nods, probably more than he should. "She'll be pleased that you asked for her."

NINE

Seth

October 1, 1992

Dear Notebook,

I can't stop reading about that plane that crashed in Nepal this week. I went to a pawnshop and got a wrecked old TV so I can watch the news now too. It crashed right into a mountain. Everyone killed—167 people. Just bam and no more them. Like my family. I wonder if there was anyone like me. Maybe someone who didn't get on the plane with the rest of their family. Left behind like me. Wondering why. Weird but it was the same airport that had another really big crash in July. Dr Whitmore told me I shouldn't dwell on negative things like this. It's what he calls unhealthy. He thinks I'm making good progress but I hope you never read this Dr W because the truth is I don't tell you half of it. It wouldn't help.

There is some good stuff for a change. Prof Altimari likes my work. She's fantastic. Her thing is sculpture, and she has a weird 3D way of looking at

stuff that blows my mind. What she knows and sees—
I think it could help me a lot. She started working
with me during class and said I could come for extra
help if I wanted to. I'll be meeting with her Monday
for the first time. I haven't felt excited about anything
like I do about this since before the fire. Karen has
been seeing her for help for a couple of weeks now.
Karen works right next to me in class so I know she
was really good to start with and her work is improv-
ing already.

Painting makes me feel alive for a while even though
really I'm just dead inside most of the time. The thing
is it doesn't feel all that good to be alive. It's like being
wide awake with the flu or something. You're better off
sleeping through it and waking up when you're better. I
would do that if I was sure I would get better.

TEN

CATHERINE

Trembling, hot all over, nauseated, Catherine pulls herself up from the depths of a nightmare. Far too many similar experiences tell her that if she looks in the mirror, her cheeks will be flushed. The dreams are back, and she had hoped—would have prayed if she believed there was anyone to pray to—that they'd been gone for good.

Trying to sleep right now is worse than pointless, so she gets up and finds her robe. She'll need it when the evaporating perspiration brings a chill to her hot skin. She fills a large glass with water and takes it to the window, where a few shreds of cloud show the faintest traces of predawn light. The sun won't be up for a long time, so she sits on the couch, leans her head back, and holds the cool glass to her forehead.

If only she'd been smarter, more aware of what was going on. Seth wasn't the first confused or troubled student she'd ever taught. He might have been the first, though, who was so deeply talented as well. His demons, whatever they were, had informed his work, and unlike so many young students who had both the desire to say something important and the skills to do it, he had something real to say. There was nothing of the newly postadolescent about the emotions his work evoked. His paintings could be thrilling and painful, hard to take yet leaving you wanting more.

And Seth had been far from her first student who needed extra guidance, nor was he the first she'd given it to. She had helped him after class hours and watched him grow. He was never at a loss for expressing sadness or terror with paint, charcoal, pencil, or clay, but she couldn't say the same for words. Even after months, she'd learned precious little about what ugly thing in his life had made him who he was. That came later. If only she'd known more. Before . . . She'd tried to help, but it must have been too late. Or too little. Or maybe the whole debacle was her fault, plain and simple, because she couldn't draw a line that needed drawing. She'll never know. She has to learn to accept that.

Catherine sits opposite Stefano Tosi, one of Italy's most respected experts in bronze casting. She's managed to do enough work to appear functional and legitimate, although most of it was from before the nightmares reappeared. Even if he did have other business along the way, Catherine appreciates his driving fourteen hours from Florence to see her. As a graduate student, she'd taken two of his courses and always hoped to work with him again. Now he sits in her studio, his back to the west doors. Judging from the fit, his charcoal suit, so at odds with the dirty hard-work nature of what he does, must be custom made. When he moves his arm, the sunlight shoots glints from his cuff links all around the space. His hair is salt-and-pepper now, making him even more distinguished, and his beard and mustache appear to have been trimmed at most half an hour ago. Even seated on these stools, legs crossed, the heel of one stylish black-leather boot hooked in perfect pose on the foot ring, Stefano manages to look elegant. Their conversation today has been satisfying and productive. Planning the next steps is under way.

"I am happy to hear you still love Firenze, because I may very well have some projects we can work on together in the future. Does that interest you, Catherine?"

"Very much. I even have some drawings I'll show you. Some ideas we might collaborate on."

"Excellent. I can help you find an apartment there and help you get settled in when—if—the time comes. I think the stimulation and excitement of the city would be good for you after your nice vacation here. I think you will be very happy living again in Florence."

"That does sound wonderful, and I can't wait to see your studio. Next month should be good. Right now, though, let me get those drawings." Catherine goes over to a neighboring table and pushes piles of papers and drawings aside. "I don't understand. They were right here last night."

"What I have in mind would be some bronzes. There is a *museo*—a big one—who wants reproductions of some fine works. And you would be suited to this, I think. And very pleased with the works when I am able to tell you about them. But for now . . ." He presses a finger to his lips.

"Of course. I understand." Catherine gives up on shuffling papers and moving sketch pads. Defeated, she tries to think of what to say about them. She's not the neatest or most organized person in the world, and Stefano knows that. But she doesn't want him to chalk this up to utter carelessness after he's come so far to see her.

She's about to apologize when Stefano stands. "I'm afraid I have to go. But don't worry. It can't be easy working in a strange space. I think you have accomplished a great deal in a short time here. You can bring the drawings with you to Florence next month."

"I guess I'll have to. With luck, I'll have more plans ready to go then too. Or at least ready for you to critique."

"Excellent. And we should—"

Behind Stefano, something catches Catherine's eye, and she leans around him to spy the boy, standing silently a short distance away. She smiles. How long has he been there? She looks back to Stefano.

"Sorry, but a little friend of mine has come in. He's behind you."

Stefano turns and looks. "Where?"

When she looks past Stefano's shoulders again, the boy is gone. She can't tell if she's more flustered by the missing drawings or by what surely must seem like her imagination running wild. "He must have run out."

Stefano doesn't seem concerned, so she acts as if nothing has happened. "Let me walk you to your car."

After wishing Stefano a safe trip, she returns to the barn, determined to find the drawings. In the middle of her methodical search of the table, she hears a rustling sound in one of the darker corners of the barn. When she looks up, she's shocked to see a tiny snowstorm of large, irregular white flakes floating down onto the floor. Catherine knows without even looking at them that they are her drawings. She gathers up the shredded remnants and looks up at the network of beams, rafters, and partial lofts. It's hard to tell for sure where the papers could have come from—there are so many nooks and crannies, so many possibilities. And standing very still, holding her breath, she hears sounds, tiny sounds that could be mice or rats or birds—or who knows what lives here?

She takes the papers to a table and examines them. They appear to have been clawed to bits. Or perhaps bitten. It had to have been an animal. It must have been. Although how the animal got the papers is something of a mystery. Or maybe it had been the child. He might have seen something he liked about them and taken them, leaving them in a spot that some sharp-clawed creature had discovered. Or, it's possible—could he have overheard her say she wanted to show them to Stefano and felt jealous? In any case, the pile of paper bits is not in any way useful, so she scoops up the entire mess and brings it to the trash can against the far wall. When she turns back, the boy is standing in front of her.

"Holy——! Where did you come from?" She places a hand to her chest to still her flip-flopping heart. "Did you do that?" She points to the trash barrel. Her voice is gentle. She's far more puzzled than angry.

He does not react in any way, and when Catherine hears a fluttering sound, she turns and sees behind her a single drawing sailing down from the rafters, riding a lazy zigzag on the soft breeze. When she looks back to the boy, he is, as she knew he would be, no longer there.

ELEVEN

SETH

October 13, 1992

Dear Notebook,

I don't know how I got so lucky that someone as good as Professor Altimari is interested in my work. How is that even possible? She opens up the studio after class hours and works with me one-on-one. It makes such a big difference. She asked us to call her by her first name too. That's pretty cool but it's hard to get used to thinking of her as Catherine. I can't believe that she actually likes what I do. Yeah, she gets it. I don't even know what to say about that. She just encourages me to let go and work free. I'm doing stuff I never would even try without her.

But it stirs things up. Dr Whitmore thinks stuff like that is great. And when I tell him about it next month—if I go—I know what he'll say. Yada yada yada, it makes me face things. Bullshit. I face it all the time. I can't get away from it. I wonder what he'd say if

I told him sometimes, I suddenly smell the fire. It happens once a day. At least. And the dreams won't stop. The only good part is that in the dream sometimes it seems like the end is going to be different—like I'll go home a day later or a week later. The worst is when it seems like I'm almost about to figure out what's going on, like I know what's coming. Because then I feel like maybe I can stop it before it happens. But it never works out. I'm sitting there at dinner with them—Mom, Dad, Amy. The kitchen looks totally normal. And I'm thinking, yeah, so we know you all die in a fire, right? But there's time. Isn't there? We can stop it. And I know they know too. They know they don't have long to live and it doesn't even seem like they think it's wrong or anything. It's just the way it is. I'm always trying to think how to stop it and they all seem to feel sorry for me. Them feeling sorry for me. That's plain crazy.

There was another big plane crash. This one slammed right into an apartment building in Amsterdam. Two engines fell off the damn wing, and the pilot lost control. What the hell? One engine falling off a wing is already pretty damn freakish, but two? 43 people dead. The whole world is like one big Stephen King story. Like there's a laughing clown out there somewhere in charge of all this shit.

By the way, Notebook, if you were paying attention, you saw I slipped something in up there. Yeah. I'm thinking of taking a vacation from the meds and Whitmore. Dr W isn't a bad guy. But I don't feel like he's helping me much. I'm not sure he really gets me or what's going on. Prof Alti Catherine does. If art is so good for me, why not try that? Art therapy is a big thing now, right? So I'll be my own therapist. Especially if Catherine can help me.

Total dead since I started keeping track

Plane crashes: 501

Natural disasters: 2155

TWELVE

CATHERINE

It had been a harrowing night of dreams and self-recriminations, and today Catherine has renewed her determination to move forward, concentrating on good things. On the list of positives is yesterday's tantalizing offer from Stefano and Mark's return from the road tomorrow. But it's the prospect of seeing the boy again today that excites her most. Still somewhat spooked by yesterday's incident with the shredded drawings, she's decided that a bird of some kind must have stolen her drawings, the way that crows steal shiny things. For their nests or whatever it is birds do. She'll have to remember to ask Giulia about it.

Right now, she's in a small market in the center of Macri to pick up a few necessities. The wood floor is worn into irregular undulations, throwing Catherine a hair off-kilter as she walks around, much as if she were on a boat. She is looking at a bin of outsize yellow fruits thinking, *Lemon, orange, or grapefruit?* when a woman pushing a stroller stops beside her. "They're lemons. Hard to believe, isn't it?" Her smile is mellow, warm, and amused. "Hi, I'm Sandra. You must be Giulia's new guest."

"Hi." How does she know? "Yes. And I guess I'm—well, glaringly American."

She laughs. "It was only a matter of time until we ran into each other. I know everyone who shops here, and you're new. Plus, the monster lemon has thrown you for a loop, so I figured you haven't been here all that long."

"You're right. I'm Catherine." She squeezes to the side of the narrow aisle to let another shopper pass. "Do you know Giulia?"

"I do. For several years now. In fact, she told me all about you, and I've been meaning to get in touch and invite you and your husband to join my husband and me for dinner one evening. American expats in Macri—not a very big group, so it might be nice to trade notes."

"That sounds lovely, although we're hardly what you'd call expats."

"Well, who knows?" She smiles. "Maybe you're expats in the making. We didn't start out intending to stay, but here we are."

"Where are you from?"

"Originally from Iowa. Yeah, I come by this corn-fed look honestly. But in my heart, I feel like I've always been from right here." She leans over the baby in the stroller and blocks her enthusiastic attempts to pull packets of bright-colored sponges from the shelves. She straightens back up. "We came on our honeymoon the first time. With a tour group—you know, as many cities as you can cram into a week and still have some hope of knowing where you are?"

Catherine laughs. "And they came here?"

"Oh, heavens no! But we did, the next year. An anniversary trip. And that's when I fell in love with the figs."

"Sounds like there's a story here."

"Oh, there is. But I truly have to go right now. Listen, can I give you a call tomorrow? We can work out a time for you and your husband to come over, and we'll tell you all about it over dinner, OK?"

"Um—sure. You'll have to call me at the main house because—"

"I know. No phone in the guesthouse. Would around eleven tomorrow be good?"

"Sure." The two women walk through the four aisles together. The modern stroller is far too wide for the space, yet every customer makes way for it. As Catherine has noticed before in other small Italian towns, a parent with a stroller, usually a mother, receives singular deference, something just this side of royalty. Catherine stops, looking at a display of cookies.

"I don't know if you're a fan of hazelnuts or not, but these—" Sandra picks up a red box and leans in to whisper. "These are the devil's own cookies."

Catherine studies the cookies and on impulse puts two boxes into her small wagon.

There is a curious note of conspiracy in Sandra's smile. "I think you'll be glad you got those." She leans down to offer a pacifier to the baby, who has started to fuss. "Valeria, sweet, it's OK. We're leaving now." She turns to Catherine. "Talk to you tomorrow."

Catherine isn't sure what to make of Sandra as she watches her walk toward the front of the store or how she ended up accepting a dinner invitation from a perfect stranger. Placing her few grocery items on the ancient counter, Catherine is lost in thought when she feels a light touch on her hand. She looks to see that the improbably tiny elderly woman behind the counter wants her attention. Her smile is wide and approving as she holds up one of the red boxes of cookies and nods her head in enthusiastic approval. Patting Catherine's hand, she squeezes it once before continuing to add up the items. Why is anyone so interested in her shopping choices? Oh well, it's one of the things about life in a tiny village that must take some getting used to.

◆ ◆ ◆

Carrying a large tray out to the studio, Catherine is armed with coffee, fruit, a sandwich, and some of the cookies she bought that morning. She's not at all sure what came over her, buying two boxes. Wisely, she's left all but two of the chocolate-hazelnut biscuits in the kitchen.

Catherine is reshaping the armature for a small statue when a soft scuffling catches her attention. Heart pounding, she turns all the way around to find the boy watching her. She stays casual, smiling once and returning to work. Under her breath she says, "Why are you always behind me, huh?" and her heart races again when she sees him, in her peripheral vision, move up closer, the closest he has ever come. Again she smiles and nods once toward a stool before ignoring him, or at least appearing to ignore him. When he sits on the floor, cross-legged and cautious, she gives a silent cheer. He's the butterfly landing on her finger, the fawn eating from her hand. She can be patient. She works in quiet.

After an exhausting hour of studied nonchalance, Catherine puts down the armature, and without looking at her silent companion, walks to the tray for a cookie. She bites one, says "Mmmmm," and holds out the remaining cookie to the child. Cocking her head and raising her eyebrows in what she hopes is a universal gesture for "OK?" she walks slowly toward him, holding out the cookie. He accepts it, eating quickly, never taking his eyes from hers. Victory!

"You're not so strange, are you? You're just a little boy who likes cookies. Right?" There's no reply. "Well, you'll be ready to talk soon, I think." She holds up one finger. "*Un momento, per favore*, I have more. In the house. Wait for me!"

Once in the kitchen, she grabs the open box and pours a small glass of milk, watching the barn to make sure the boy doesn't leave. But when she returns—when she walks back into the studio saying, "Here I am!"—she's not all that surprised that he is nowhere to be seen.

◆　◆　◆

Catherine knocks on Giulia's back door. "Ciao! It's Catherine."

"Let yourself in." Giulia's voice carries over the sound of Pippo's excited barking.

"You look busy." Catherine takes in the open accounting books on the sideboard, the pasta drying on racks, and the jumble of dishes in the sink.

"It is always like this. The work of a farm is never finished. The work of a house is never finished. So, me? I am two times never finished."

Placing a covered plate on the table, Catherine picks up a toy and plays tug with an ever-enthusiastic Pippo. "I thought he was getting adopted weeks ago."

"I thought this too. Maybe he will go. Maybe he will stay here. These things . . . must be exactly right to work out."

Pippo settles on top of Catherine's feet. "I baked some biscotti. I added pistachios to that recipe from last time. I hope they came out OK."

"You are comfortable now to try new things. That's very good!" Giulia sits at the table. "The espresso—two minutes."

On the table, a pale-yellow ceramic bowl overflows with eggs in assorted shades of blue-greens and creams. "I keep meaning to ask about your eggs—such unusual colors."

"Not the kind you see in the market. My baby brother—he keeps chickens and gives me these eggs. *Mamma* used to have chickens here, but one day, she said she had enough. I miss them."

"I'd love to do that. If I were going to be here longer."

"Well—who can say, eh?" Giulia smiles and holds Catherine's gaze until a sound catches the attention of both. Assunta, a red-checked apron over her usual black dress, stands in the doorway. Giulia said Assunta wore black to show mourning and respect for someone who had died. Asked who, Giulia said, "Is always someone, no?"

"I can teach you all about the chickens." Assunta leans on the table as she sits. "Today, though, we learn more about the oven."

Giulia pours espresso into tiny black-and-red floral cups. "Mark is back today?"

"Right before dinnertime."

"I think you miss him. You are in the barn all the time."

"I do, but I need to work too. You know, though, I wanted to ask you something about that—about the barn. The young boy I mentioned the first day? He visits me there a lot. You haven't thought of anyone, have you? Children nearby?"

"I'm afraid not me. *Mamma?*" Should Catherine read something into the look Giulia exchanges with Assunta?

Assunta shrugs. "Maybe one kilometer away there is a girl—very small. She comes to visit her *nonna.*"

"I'm so curious, and he won't talk to me at all. But the strangest part is how he sneaks up and disappears suddenly. Every time."

"Children! They are like puppies."

"I suppose." Catherine reaches down to pet Pippo. "He's very serious, but I find him charming."

"How lucky, then, he has come to visit you." Again, that quick glance between Giulia and Assunta. Catherine is about to ask about it when Assunta stands up.

"Time for the lesson. Today we make *scardellini.* Or maybe you hear of this cookie with another name—*Ossa di morto.*"

"Bones of the dead?"

"They are a favorite in our family." Assunta hands an apron to Catherine. "Old, old recipe. But you must be careful when you eat them! They are very—mmm—*duri*—Giulia?"

"Hard, *Mamma.* They are very hard. Tough."

"Like the rocks. And you must dip them in the *caffè* or the *vino* for the safe chewing."

Catherine laughs.

"This is true." Giulia somehow finds room for the cups in the sink. "These dead people and their bones—you must be careful!" And she turns to Catherine and smiles.

THIRTEEN

SETH

November 10, 1992

Dear Notebook,

Another plane crash in Indonesia. 31 people dead because they were going on vacation or something. 423 people killed in a huge storm in Sri Lanka. It lasted 7 days, but that's still a lot of people. And then this family upstate—a meteor hit their car. Can you even believe it? Thirty pounds of space junk manages to find its way to Earth and zero in on some family's car to smash. You can't tell me that's something that could happen in a rational world. It's plain fucked up.

Dr W says a month is a long time to be thinking about a meteor. I told him about my planned vacation from him and he didn't like it. He wants to at least "stay connected" so I said I'd call him in a month and yeah maybe I will. I've been off the meds for a week now and I feel a whole lot better. Not dizzy. I can think clearly too. Food looks better. Like something I want to eat, not have to choke down. I just feel *clean*.

I'll miss having someone to talk to but what's the point if he doesn't get it? I think Catherine might be someone I could really talk to. She gets stuff. She sees the world a lot like I do. I think we could be friends. I think maybe we already are a little bit.

That meteor thing has been making the nightmares even worse. That's why I'm up writing at 3:17 a.m. Not sleeping is better than killing my family over and over again.

Oh, yeah, Dr W assures me—used to assure me—I did not kill my family. Well how the hell does he know? You want to tell me that? Because

a) they are all dead

b) I am not dead

c) it was my fault they didn't get out

d) he wasn't the fuck there

You can say what you want but it was my fault. Though the nice thing about you, Notebook, is that you don't say much. No telling me that it wasn't on purpose, that I couldn't have known. All that means is I'm not an *evil* shit. Yeah, there's something for my tombstone. A real achievement. I'm still a shit, though. And you know what? Who's even left to put anything on my tombstone at all? What do people like me do? Preorder I guess. And ask the guy with the chisel to fill in the date. The rest kind of feels like it's over already.

New total dead people

Plane crashes: 532

Natural disasters: 2578

FOURTEEN

MARK

The drive to the saltworks runs through a spectacular world of bleached neutrals and shimmering blues. Everywhere along the gritty, narrow, glaring-white road, huge mounds of crystal salt sit drying in the sun. Creative arrangements of terra-cotta tiles form provisional roofs protecting the salt dunes from dirt and rain. Hugging the shore of this portion of the lagoon is a sweeping network of rectangular pools—the salt pans. The shallow seawater within them ranges in shade from white to deep blue and, here and there, an occasional, surprising pink. Fifteenth-century Dutch-style windmills, their cream-colored bodies sporting orange conical hats, their trapezoidal wings of metallic mesh long stripped of canvas, dot the landscape. Once the mills exploited the steady winds to pump water and grind salt. Now they simply stand as a gracious reminder of a heritage, the enduring connection between this tiny sliver of coast and the labor-intensive gleaning of the salt.

A reluctant Mark pulls into a small, sandy parking area. The wind here is fragrant, the salt smell mingling with the piquant aroma of herbs that grow in every crack and cranny. "It's unbelievable out here, but—Museum of Salt? I hope Giulia's right, that this is interesting, because the name is deadly."

"She hasn't steered us wrong yet."

"I guess capturing salt does sound moderately adventurous."

"Yeah, that was a funny word." Catherine walks to the edge of one of the pans. A strong breeze, the steady, warm breath of the African desert, rushes off the water. The brilliant sun flicks thousands of silvery glints from the gently crinkled surface. "Mark, look. These little stone borders—they're what we saw that guy walking on."

Mark squats to examine the nearest edge. "These pans are like giant swimming pools. And nothing but that long edging between them. I wonder why so narrow."

"Let's go inside and find out." Catherine taps Mark's shoulder, and he teeters, balancing himself with a palm to the ground before springing up and throwing an arm over Catherine's shoulders as they head for the low rectangular building attached to one of the windmills.

They pull open the heavy door and duck to enter. All around on the walls of the rustic stone interior are black-and-white photographs of men laboring in the blazing heat. Antique tools, enormous cogs, and assorted pieces of machinery fill the open spaces of the floor. At a table in the back corner a young Sicilian woman sits. She explains that the salt "factory" has been in her family for many generations, and she offers a tour in what might be the most winning Italian-inflected English Mark has ever heard.

When they emerge back out into the bright afternoon, Mark is the saltworks' newest fan. The age of the process alone is astonishing. The Phoenicians started it. The Carthaginians, Romans, and Moors continued it. And they do it more or less the same way today. It's humbling to think that the windmills he considered ancient are the "new" ones, with the long-gone originals dating from almost twelve hundred years ago. It's such a simple idea: pump water from one shallow pan to the next as evaporation progresses, teasing salt from the sea in a long, arduous process. *Captured* may be the word, after all.

Mark again squats at the water's edge. "So the narrow edges make it easier to get the salt and water from one pan to the next."

"My favorite thing is how the color changes as the water evaporates. Amazing. And the pink!"

"She did say algae, right? Crazy." He stands up and stretches. "This was phenomenal. I thought the best part was going up into the windmill, though. The angles, the view. Those mills own their space."

Catherine puts her arms around his waist. "I don't even know how to say it. The way of life here—it goes back so far that it seems—I don't know—more real. More genuine, maybe. How far does this feel from pushing your way through Dean & DeLuca and paying ten times the price for your 'Artisanal Sea Salt' in a fancy jar? This"—she holds up her hand-packed bag of salt crystals—"was done for locals—friends and family."

He loves seeing Catherine caught up in the romance of an idea. He knows it will show up in her work. And he just plain loves seeing her happy. "Hey, Cath, I have an idea."

"Better than standing here?"

"Want to go out for a walk on the water, so to speak?"

Catherine looks at the long, slim strips of stone that taper to points in the distance. "Promise not to push me in?" Her voice is playful.

Mark responds in kind. "You did come close to pushing me in before."

"That was an accident. Mostly."

"Well, you know I'm easy to knock off balance. Anyway, if you don't trust me, walk behind me."

"Perfect." Catherine steps behind him, and they set out along a narrow strip.

After a minute, Mark stops and speaks over his shoulder. "You know, you can't pass me out there, so you're in front on the way back. However you look at it, sooner or later, you have to trust me."

◆ ◆ ◆

A young man seats Mark and Catherine in the center of the large, open marble-floored restaurant. Although the parking lot is full, only one in every three or four tables is occupied—puzzling Mark before he notes a series of heavy double doors set into the back wall. It must be a private room—a big one, judging from the number of doors. When he listens, he realizes that muffled voices and laughter suggest a sizable party is taking place there right now.

Busy with her menu, Catherine seems unaware of any of this. The waiter, placing a basket of bread on the table, says, "Very hot. From the oven." He pours deep-green olive oil into a red clay dish. "Would you care for wine?" They order the house red and the waiter leaves.

"How do they always know we speak English?" Mark tears off a piece of the warm semolina bread.

"You're kidding, right? We don't look local at all. Plus the guy who seated us probably heard us talking and told the waiter."

"Possible. But the clothes you're wearing now make you look like a local to me."

"Oh, thanks. You noticed!" Catherine pinches and lifts the shoulders of her cobalt-blue-and-hot-orange blouse, looking at the fabric with obvious satisfaction. She lets go and smooths the lace trim with care. "This lace is handmade. I look maybe a smidge more authentic, now, right?"

"Yeah." Mark takes a bite of bread. "If that's what you're after."

"I am." She returns to her menu. "You know what sounds great? This *risotto con i funghi.*"

"I know it's unsophisticated of me, but I can't get behind a food called *funghi.* It's like funky and fungus put together."

"Even if it means 'very delicious mushrooms'? Loosely translated."

"Even if. But I might taste yours if you get it."

Fifteen minutes later, their orders placed, Catherine and Mark are sipping wine when two men and two women, dressed for a party and carrying wrapped gifts, walk through the restaurant to one of the doors in back. When they open the door, the sound of happy chatter and laughter pours out. Along with it comes a toddler, a small boy wearing blue-satin shorts and a white sailor shirt. He runs shrieking and giggling through the center of the restaurant as a woman who must be his mother—slowed to a near crawl by her fitted dress and spike heels—attempts an ineffectual pursuit.

"Mark?" Catherine widens her eyes. "Should we—"

"Yep."

And he is up and halfway to the child when it occurs to him that the boy's father could walk in, misunderstand what he sees, and deck Mark first, asking questions later. But he reaches the child and offers a gentle hand, taking him to his teetering mother. She thanks Mark with many excited words, most of which he can't understand, before scooping the child up and mincing her excruciating way back to the party.

Mark sits. "I was desperately trying to figure out how to say, 'I am not a bad guy,' but fortunately, I didn't need to."

"I don't think it's like that so much here. People take an interest in each other's kids, and no one thinks it's weird or threatening. Much better than home. Like so many things here."

"Yeah, but this place—it's great, but it has its problems. I haven't been to a meeting yet that came off on time. I don't know how they stand it. Or get anything done."

"Now, Mark, we discussed the time thing. Should we do the math again?"

Mark pats her hand. "I'd rather tell you about the most amazing place I visited on the way back here. In Riposto."

As Mark describes last week's visit, one of the back doors opens bit by bit, giving the impression of moving on its own until two little girls in elaborate dresses peek out. Holding hands, they steal away from the party and walk through the restaurant, a pair of five-year-old generals inspecting the troops, pointing at tables, and chattering along the way. Catherine is speaking when the girls pass by, and the children giggle.

"We must sound odd to them."

"Or they're judging our taste in wine." Mark refills their glasses.

The girls reach the front of the restaurant, and the taller one bends to whisper into the ear of her companion. They walk back toward the table and stop, looking first at Mark, then at Catherine, swinging their still-joined hands. Their burst of rapid Italian runs right over Mark's head, and judging from the look on Catherine's face, she isn't doing much better. But she smiles and replies in slow Italian. The girls become suddenly shy and laugh before they run away and regroup. They repeat this several times—each time, Catherine tries to answer their questions; each time, they run off.

"What are they saying, Cath?"

"I'm not really sure. It's so fast. And they speak—you know—like kids. And in Italian. But I think they started out curious about where we're from, and now they can't fathom that we don't speak Italian as well as they do. They're a riot."

A moment later, the girls are on the way back, two boys along with them, one several years younger and one several years older. Catherine looks pleasantly surprised at first, but then seems disappointed. The older boy greets them with polite English while the younger boy studies Mark and Catherine as if he believes he is invisible.

"Do you study English at school?" Catherine says.

"Yes, signora. They are too young, these three." He explains that he and the others, all cousins, are here for yet another cousin's birthday. "Angelica and Maria—they are silly. And not too polite. They want to hear how you sound. Like in the movies, maybe, they think. Or the TV. But now, they will stop bothering you because almost the cake of the party is ready for the eating. If their *mammas* see they are not sitting there—" He raises his hand to his mouth and bites the side of his index finger in an *I'll get you* gesture that causes the girls to giggle. He turns and speaks to them, and they curtsy and run off, taking the littlest one with them. Before leaving, the older boy bows from the waist. "I hope you will enjoy to stay on our Sicilian island."

Mark grins. "That was hilarious. We had our own mini paparazzi there."

"Right? I kind of like being a celebrity. Even if our fan club is three five-year-olds and their ten-year-old keeper."

"When you first saw the boys, what was that look on your face?"

"Oh. Did I have a look? I thought I recognized one of them at first, but I was wrong."

"We must look ridiculous if Giulia is watching right now." Catherine struggles with her end of the kayak as she and Mark make their way from the house to the water's edge. Despite their almost-comical clumsiness, they get the banana-colored boat into the water, and after some discussion of proper paddling technique, set off to explore the lagoon. The warm wind blows a few strands of hair into Catherine's eyes, and Mark wishes he had a free hand to brush them away. It doesn't take much to spur his desire to do something for her, to keep all the badness and sadness away from her forever.

"Now, remember what Giulia said." He looks stern. "Don't let the bottom of *the ship* touch the ground."

"I knew it wasn't deep, but this is crazy." Catherine dips a hand into the water. "And I caught that 'ship.' It makes me wonder what wildly inappropriate Italian words I throw around every day."

"Let's try to stay in the deeper part. Like over two feet."

"Aye-aye, Captain." Catherine salutes and nearly loses one of her paddles.

"Why am I the captain?"

"Because the captain goes down with the ship, silly."

"The only way I could drown on this 'voyage' is to fall unconscious. *Facedown.*"

Catherine looks over the side. "What's that?" She points with one oar. "It's awfully straight to be natural."

A long stone structure shimmers and wriggles beneath the clear water. It seems to continue as far as Mark can see. "No idea. Another question for Giulia."

They row awhile in silence before Catherine says, "You want to finish telling me about that place in Riposto?"

"Sure. Let's see. I told you about Roberto. Well, his land—and there's a lot of it—is beautiful. 'Beautiful' with a capital *B*. Hell, I don't know, maybe *all* capitals. Views of the sea in one direction and views of Mount Etna in the other."

"Must be amazing."

"And I mean *views*. It was honestly one of the most spectacular settings I've ever seen. It would make a great *agriturismo*. I'd love to see him be able to subsidize his lemon orchard that way."

"Mmmm. Lemon orchard. Must smell heavenly."

"It does. And he's a nice guy. Raising two kids by himself. His mother helps."

"That reminds me. I keep meaning to tell you about something that's been happening to me."

Mark stops rowing. "*Happening* to you? Are you OK?"

"I'm fine. Just row. This is something kind of fun. That boy I saw watching us when we were looking at the studio? Well, he's come back a half-dozen times, maybe more. Four years old, I'd say. Five, tops. He comes to the studio and watches me. I love that he keeps me company, but he's like a little phantom. I never see him arrive, and I never see him leave."

"Can't you, you know, keep your eye on him? Once he's there?"

"I know, right? That's what's so intriguing. I try to do that and I lose him anyway. The barn *is* enormous, and it has a lot of dark areas, but still. He even disappeared when I tried to point him out to Stefano Tosi."

"Disappeared?"

"Not like poof away or anything. But he manages to *be gone* somehow."

"Well, I'm home for a few days now. There'll be two of us to figure out where he goes. I think we can get to the bottom of it."

"I hope so. I'd like that."

Mark sits next to Catherine on Sandra and Kenneth's couch. Dinner was pleasant enough, and now they wait while their hosts put the kids to bed. The evening has been a little awkward, but it's important for Catherine to spend some time with other people, and she and Sandra seem to be hitting it off. Sandra's some kind of writer, although she's been a little cagey about specifics. But she does seem to understand the kind of work life Catherine leads.

"I guess they really like coral." Mark keeps his voice low as he points to a collection of half a dozen dark-edged, deep frames on the nearest wall. Each contains a coral branch, a tiny window framing a miniature coral tree. "What do you call those kinds of frames?"

"Shadow boxes, I think. That really red coral is common around here. Great color."

Sandra returns from upstairs. "Valeria is already asleep. Claudio is reading in bed, and Kenneth should be down in a minute." She sits and curls her legs underneath her. "Claudio's nearly nine now and thinks he should pick his own bedtime—like midnight. But he'll be unconscious in fifteen minutes."

"I predict ten." Kenneth returns and sits. "He's trying hard, but he's losing the battle."

"Did you change Claudio's name when you moved here, or do you just like Italian names? I love that name, by the way. Mark can tell you I'm crazy about Italian names." Mark smiles to himself at Catherine's clumsy attempt to make sure her question wasn't insulting.

"Oh, no." Sandra's smile is serene. "We adopted Claudio and Valeria here—together."

"I didn't realize they were adopted. Not that it matters." Catherine is squirming in her chair now. "So, they are biological brother and sister?"

"They aren't." Sandra reaches for a chocolate from a bowl on the coffee table. "But they both needed a home, and it seemed to make sense. Giulia helped us."

"Giulia?" Catherine looks to Mark. He isn't sure what to say, so he says nothing.

"She helped us with a private arrangement. She knows everybody and everything. We stayed in the cottage you're in when we first came here. Giulia and Assunta couldn't have been nicer."

"I was wondering how you knew we didn't have a phone."

"What about you guys?" Sandra passes the bowl of candy. "Do you want kids someday?"

It irks Mark, as it always does, when someone invades his personal space with that question. What makes them think that's acceptable?

"Mark and I have certainly talked about it, but no conclusions yet."

"Oh, understood. I hope you don't feel I was prying."

Mark can't imagine what else you would call it, and his irritation is growing. "Well, why would we think that, Sandra?" He feels a little bad when Catherine shoots him what can only be called the evil eye. Maybe he shouldn't have been quite so sarcastic, but either Sandra didn't catch it, didn't care, or is unnaturally controlled. His money is on the latter.

Mark stands. "Hey, I just noticed the time. We really need to get going. Right, Cath? I have an early-morning meeting in Palermo." He gives Catherine a look he's pretty sure she gets, since her agreement is prompt and convincing. In the car on the way home, however, she wants to know why.

"Really? They were a little creepy, don't you think? So—calm. Especially Sandra. And she's weirdly smiley."

"They were a little stiff, but they seemed like nice people."

"Well, if you're going to be spending time with Sandra, maybe you can find out more about how Giulia helped them buy the kids."

"Isn't that a little strong? Giulia probably knows the families of all the unmarried pregnant girls around here and works out good homes for their children."

"Yeah? Claudio was at least five or six when they adopted him. So Giulia must know 'young girls' who are tired of their kids too."

FIFTEEN

CATHERINE

Catherine walks into the studio and takes in a sharp breath at the sight of someone sitting on one of her stools. It's the boy, wearing the same clothes he always wears, his face as solemn as it always is. She approaches the table, slow and tentative, and sits next to him.

"Have you been here all morning?"

He doesn't answer.

"All night?" She leans in a bit closer. "Are you hungry?"

Catherine holds out the pastry she's brought along for a midmorning snack. He accepts it. "You are a mystery." Picking up pad and charcoal, she resumes work on a sketch in progress, pleased that he hasn't left. Yet.

She's almost finished the sketch, and he hasn't moved. "So do you have a name?" She stops drawing and peeks at him, hoping she looks friendly and interested, not creepy and prying. The boy reaches over and takes the charcoal from her hand. She can feel her heart pound, but she keeps her expression steady. Holding the charcoal in his fist the way a toddler might, he writes a letter *N* on the desk. He looks up at her, and she nods encouragement. Head down, his strokes slow and deliberate, he adds *I C O*. The charcoal breaks with a snap at the last second, and he freezes, fearful eyes darting up to hers, body tensed to run.

"It's OK. Don't worry." Catherine reaches out to touch his arm, but he backs away, so she stops. She points to the letters on the desk. "Is that your name—Nico?"

He doesn't react.

"Well, I think it must be. Do you like to write, Nico? Or draw?" At the adjacent table, she picks up a large pad and scouts around in a box of jumbled supplies. "I have some pastels—crayons—here. Pretty colors. And a pad for your own." She pulls the pastels from the box. "Would you like that?" But when she looks up, the stool is empty, and Nico is nowhere in sight.

Catherine places the pad and pastels near the spot where the boy— Nico!—sat. A wide charcoal smudge is all that remains of the simple letters he'd written on the table.

"Morning, Cath." Mark comes in carrying two cups of coffee. Catherine runs her hand over the charcoal smear. "Did you see him?"

"Who?"

"Nico. The boy."

"You know his name now?"

"You didn't pass him on the way in?"

"From your question, I guess I just missed him."

Over the last several days, Catherine has felt Nico growing less wary, even if he still manages—every time—to be gone when Mark arrives. Now Nico sits on the floor near Catherine, who is working in clay. Nico watches with what appears to be real interest, going so far as to approach at one point to touch the unused clay. The way he'd patted it with his whole hand and the hint of satisfaction on his face had been endearing, and the rush of tenderness she felt toward him had caught her off guard. Still, encouraging him to do more hasn't been working, and he won't answer any questions. Maybe he has no voice.

Catherine reaches over for more clay and cuts off a very small piece, which she softens in her hand. Walking slowly to Nico, she holds it out to him. "For you." She waits, exhaling only when he accepts it. After a few moments, he still sits, like a statue himself, clay in his fist. She makes stretching and pushing motions with her hands, then looks away to give him his space. When she glances up again, he is rolling the clay into a ball, flattening it, and rolling it again. She can feel herself beaming like a stage mother, but Nico's face remains impassive.

She brings him more clay. "Nico, can you make a statue of yourself? Can you make Nico from this clay?"

He works with care, as if he'd been waiting for her to ask. When he finishes his crude self-portrait, Catherine gives him a thumbs-up. "That's very good! Can you make me?"

Nico works the clay, producing a comical figure who, judging from the triangular shape of her lower half, is indeed Catherine in her long, loose skirt. "And now, can you make Mark? I think you know who Mark is."

Nico molds the clay into a figure of a man. Catherine places the three figures in a line and smiles. Without warning, Nico jumps up, staring at the west doors. Catherine looks but sees nothing. She remembers a cat she had as a child that would leap up from sleep and stare into an empty room, eyes wide, scaring Catherine witless.

"Do you see something, Nico? Hear something?" His eyes grow wider, and she turns again to follow his gaze, but the doorway is empty. "You're scaring me." Catherine looks back to Nico's spot on the floor, but that's empty too. The clay versions of Nico and Catherine stand side by side, but clay Mark is gone. Seconds later, Mark walks in.

Mark had thought buying toys for Nico was crazy the other day, but they're working out even better than she'd hoped. If only Mark could see for himself. He's been home for more than a week, and no luck so far in getting him to meet Nico.

Right now, Nico is playing with the farm-animal figures she's given him. He's so focused, Catherine's not sure he realizes she's sketching him. This, her third sketch of the day, would make a beautiful sculpture. "Nico?" There's that tiny thrill every time she says his name. "Do you have any brothers and sisters?" He looks up at her, expression blank, then returns to his play.

"Do you go to school yet?" She waits, then tries again. "You know your letters. Like a big boy. Or at least how to write your name. Someone must have taught you." It's eerie how he plays without making a sound or showing any trace of a smile.

"Can you tell me one thing, Nico?" She pauses until he looks at her. So! He can be curious too. "Where do you come from?" Nico returns to his toys, and Catherine is trying to think of creative ways to ask the same old questions when she hears Mark's voice outside.

"Hey, Cath? Come on out."

"Please don't go, Nico." Her voice is soft and affectionate. "Don't be afraid. Maybe some people have been mean to you, but you'll like Mark if you only give him a chance."

She goes out the door to find Mark, Giulia, and Assunta standing next to a wooden cart holding a large rocking chair, a crisscross of ropes keeping it in place. She knows she should make polite greetings, ask how Giulia is and what brings her here, but she makes a swift decision to get right to the point. "Come in, please. You can meet Nico." Giulia and Mark accompany Catherine into the barn, but Nico's spot on the floor is empty. The toys are lined up, just as she left them for him to find this morning.

"He's gone. I can't believe it." Catherine looks to the toys on the floor, then to the door. Could he be hiding someplace in a dark corner of the barn? No point speculating. She'll never find him if he is.

"I'm sorry you are so disappointed, but maybe we will cheer you up." Giulia points out the door. "We have a nice, soft chair so you do not have to sit all the time here on the hard stool. Come see."

Outside, Assunta still stands next to the cart. Catherine pats the thick corduroy fabric of the chair's seat cushion. "You didn't see him, did you, Assunta? A little boy?"

Assunta shakes her head and walks beside Catherine and Giulia into the barn as Mark carries the rocker.

"Next time," says Giulia.

Mark sets the rocker down. "He doesn't like the toys?"

"He did. He does. He cleaned up before he . . ."

"Disappeared?" says Mark. "That what you were going to say?"

"I guess."

Mark walks over to Catherine and holds her in a tight bear hug. "Are you sure you're not inhaling some fumes when you're out here? A disappearing boy—who cleans up?"

"What can I say?"

"At least he didn't take the toys with him—back to the fifth dimension."

"Mark, really. Stop. He's shy." She shakes him off.

"Sorry. I thought you'd find it funny too. Come on. Try to let it go. We both know I have to see him sooner or later."

This last round of nightmares was another of those surreal, bruising revisits to the past—the greatest hits of ghastly, Mark once called them. She'd love to wake him. The wee small hours threaten to swallow you up when you're alone. But Mark has a long drive ahead of him tomorrow. Resigned to yet another night on the couch waiting for sunrise, Catherine tucks her feet under the blanket Assunta crocheted for her and revisits events, as if one more rehash might make a difference.

Had there been some hint, early on, that she'd missed? She'd had time—all those hours they worked together when she gave him extra help, all those dark canvases filled with turmoil. But although he was never rude, he never talked about his personal life or did more than hint at some problems. She'd thought her attention would be good for him, building his self-confidence and giving him more tools he could bring to bear on canvas, paper, and clay. And it had, to some degree. She should have anticipated that he would see their time together as an invitation to be friends. And nothing was wrong with that—at first. He was endearingly awkward about it, writing what he couldn't say. The first casual notes in her mailbox, written on torn corners of notebook paper, suggested they meet for coffee after class or for lunch or for a new exhibit at MOMA or the Met. She'd always been polite and warm when she declined, saying it would not be appropriate. And maybe that was the mistake; maybe she should have left it at "No."

Then the little gifts had started, left at her office door. That had flummoxed her, and she hadn't known what to do. At Mark's suggestion, she'd ended their extra studio time together with excuses about an increased workload from the department, but she never did think he believed her.

The letters had followed, written in longhand on what looked like real stationery. Maybe he felt letters invited longer replies or conveyed more serious intent. Or it could be as simple as liking the feeling of ink on paper. There was never a whiff of anything improper or threatening about the letters—no love offered, no lust confessed, no desperation revealed. He wanted to be friends, he said, over and over, in many different and sad ways.

Could that have been it right there? Had she let him down by doing the "professional" thing when what he needed was personal support? She suspects the truth is more shameful: that she was and is so inept as a teacher—maybe as a human being—that she'd failed to recognize serious signs that anyone else would have picked up right from the start.

Catherine walks to the window. The very first moments of dawn spatter faint grains of light onto the blackness, like a handful of salt thrown onto slate. More and more grains of light appear until she can make out a dense morning mist and, enveloped in it, what looks like a small figure standing in the distance. Nico? Whoever it is stands stock-still, all color washed away in the grayness. Catherine runs out the door and to the edge of the porch. "Nico?" The figure does not move or react in any way that she can see. Wrapping the blanket around her shoulders, she sets off across the field calling "Nico! Nico!" She stops. The figure is gone, and she can't see where he might be. Unless she's imagined it. A voice behind her calls her name, and she turns to see Mark.

"What are you doing out here, Cath? The sleepwalking back?"

"No. I'm awake. I've been awake."

"Really? Because I've been out here calling you for a while now. I couldn't see, but I could hear your voice."

"A while . . . ?"

"You're shivering." Mark looks around. "Come on. Let's get inside. It's damn creepy out here. I'm half expecting Heathcliff to show up."

SIXTEEN

Seth

November 30, 1992

Dear Notebook,

Last week there was a huge fire in Windsor Castle. And a couple of days later a palace in Austria went on fire and part of it was destroyed. I guess it was the crazy clown's week to go after royalty.

The Queen was in one of their other castles when the fire started. Still, a lot of people were there and they all got out alive. People are talking about it at school. Everyone loves a castle. No one can believe how it went from some curtains on fire to out of control in fifteen minutes. I want to say yes! That happens. That's what happened to us.

I don't get how a stone castle burns really and if that went up the way it did, can you see how a wood house over a restaurant in the Bronx would go up even faster? Of course, the Queen's son didn't block everyone's way out like I did. If he did though I don't think the newspapers and TV would be saying it wasn't his fault.

I can't even count how many times I've asked myself why I picked that night to come home. I could have come home almost any weekend. What if I hadn't been such a dumb fuck and locked my room in the first place? I mean, the fire escape access was in there. I knew that. Yeah, before I went out the escape I opened my door. I did. Everyone was running around. My mother was yelling at me to get out. I saw them. My father had my sister's hand. I thought they were right behind me. But I didn't do the thing I should have. I didn't turn the lock. I never thought about wind slamming the door closed. When they didn't follow, I thought they went out the front way.

It was hell outside. Crazy hell and I couldn't get around to the front of the building. I should have just pushed past the fire crew and said I have to get to my family. I would have known they didn't get out before it was too late. I could have asked. I could have asked if they were out there. Then I would have known the fire cut off the way to the front stairs. We could have saved them. If I'd done any one of those things differently— any ONE of them—they'd all still be alive. The whole thing is my fault. It's simple logic. Saying anything else is just bullshit.

There was a lot of fire and flames and burning things in my work this week. Catherine asked me if everything is okay. I didn't know what to say so I didn't say a whole lot. Another 171 people dead in 2 plane crashes. One in Vietnam and one in China. You know people burned up on those planes. She probably thinks I'm a pyromaniac or something. I want to tell her. I want to talk to her so badly but not there in the studio where people come in and out. I need a friend, Notebook, one that talks back but doesn't pump me full of platitudes and drugs to make me supposedly feel better. Is that so much to want? It was really hard to do, but I made myself ask her if she wanted to meet for coffee. A couple of times. She said she couldn't because of her schedule. I tried asking if we could have lunch together this week and she said no, it wouldn't be "appropriate" so I thought maybe we could go to an art museum. I asked about a couple of exhibits. I really thought she'd like the Jana Sterbak show since she is so into sculpture. But she said no to all of them. Did I mention that when I say "ask" I mean I stuck notes in her office inbox? I wanted to talk to ask her in person but I couldn't do it. I can't blame her for saying no. Those notes must have looked like they came from a 10 yr old.

New total dead people

Plane crashes: 703

Natural disasters: 2578

SEVENTEEN

CATHERINE

Catherine pulls the kayak onto land and ties it to a scrubby tree. Alone in the studio all morning, all she had wanted to do was sketch the Punic ship. Coming here to Mozia should give her new inspiration and add depth to her vision of Phoenician life, making this—she assures herself—work related. And she's getting some exercise on top of it. Guilt and kayak both tucked away, she walks inland along a narrow dirt path.

Patches of thin forest mix in with areas of stone ruins, themselves often halfway covered with flowers and greenery. According to Giulia, there have been vineyards on the island for more than two hundred years. The wine, she said, is unique—pale golden in color and embodying in taste and fragrance the wild herbs that thrive on the salt air.

Catherine enters a flat, open area with ruins so casual and unkempt that the archaeological park in Marsala is Disneyland in comparison. The ground is a chaotic clutter of pottery shards and broken stone. One corner, however, has enjoyed a modicum of grooming, and she picks her way through the scattered bits of artifacts. All around her lie small jugs, ten to twelve inches high, cloaked in drifts of sandy dirt.

Scattered among the jugs are carved stone blocks a foot or so high. A few of these steles are upright, but many are down, island castaways sunning themselves in rakish poses while awaiting rescue. Steles like these generally marked something noteworthy, often a cemetery. She wishes she'd brought a sketch pad, but committing the scene to memory will have to do. Spotting a stele in better shape than most, Catherine squats, examining the relief figure of a man with his arms folded against his body. This fits with the cemetery idea, but the jugs, assuming they were for ashes, are too small.

After examining dozens of steles and jugs, she sets off toward the center of the island. She finds more woods filled with birds, more overgrown ruins, and eventually the vineyards before turning back.

At the shore near the kayak, she sits leaning back on her elbows, looking out over the water toward Macri. She feels she has discovered so much, even though she knows she has not discovered anything at all in the true sense of the word. The best finds from here are probably in local museums, yet the things you come upon yourself are always best. One pretty seashell, even if less than perfect, has more power to thrill than the most beautiful shell collection. Holding a found object brings it back to life for a short time. You appreciate it for what it is and what it was. You don't have to be the first to come upon it. Others, many others, may have encountered it before you, tossing it back at the end of the day. But that doesn't matter. What matters is the emotional bond you build with the object for the precious time it's yours.

Not everyone who has come here has "found" something exciting. Most will take the ferry, hire a guide, and visit the small museum she's heard is on the island. They won't find a thing because they have not come to this dot in the middle of the water to find, but they've come, at most, to see.

Catherine yawns. This sculpture is not going quite the way it should. Nico has been here all morning, never seeming to tire of the same hand-ful of toys. Still, she makes a mental note to buy more. She doubts he receives enrichment of any kind at home. He's absent from wherever home is for hours at a time, and no one ever comes looking for him. Are they any more attentive when he's there?

She puts the clay aside and picks up a sketch pad, her mind turn-ing back as it has all day to this week's visit to Mozia. She must make a point of getting to the Marsala Library to research the ruins. Right now, all she has are sense memories driving a powerful need to sketch.

She's on her third drawing of the area strewn with small jugs when Nico comes to stand next to her, and she glances at him while continu-ing to draw. The less attention you pay to Nico's actions, the better he likes it. She's learned that much. He's quite absorbed in watching, moving his head when he needs to for a better view. She is finishing up the sketch of the stele with the relief of the man on it when Nico lays his hand on her arm and looks at her.

With slow, deliberate motion, Nico moves his hand to her pencil, and she holds it out to him. He takes it. Catherine can still feel the tiny spots on her arm where Nico's little fingers had touched her. When he stares at her pad, she offers that as well. Nico studies the picture, takes the eraser from the benchtop, and rubs away part of the arms. He changes their angle, bringing the figure's elbows down lower toward his hips, and upper arms closer to his sides. When he hands the pad back to Catherine, she sees the drawing is imperfect, basic, as you would expect from a child. Yet his changes make sense. Are they correct? Catherine uses his structure and fills in the details as he watches, focused and intense.

"Nico?" She waits for the response she knows will not come; he continues to look at the page. "Have you seen this stone I'm drawing? Have you been there?" She turns to meet his eyes.

Nico almost—almost—smiles, and something about his expression triggers a powerful sense of what feels very much like fear, but even more like foreboding.

◆　◆　◆

The next morning, Catherine sits at a blond wood desk in a quiet corner of the library. A solicitous and efficient librarian has brought her a worn map of the ruins of Mozia. She can, she says, recommend some books, but they are from another library, and this could take quite a while—some weeks, perhaps. In the meantime, there is a bookstore in town, and Catherine can find something there to read while she waits for the more academic works. And how fortunate that right across the way from the bookstore is a shop serving the most delicious granita and gelato.

As Catherine studies the map, she sees that the area containing the steles and jugs is not only a cemetery, but a children's cemetery. What a melancholy thought—each of those small jugs filled with ashes of someone's beloved child. She feels a heavy guilt for having been there, warmed by the sun and enjoying her make-believe treasure hunt. On the verge of rolling up the map to return it, she notices a straight line leading across the water from the northern end of Mozia to the Macri area. She traces it with her finger.

The librarian, returning with a list of the requested books, glances down at the map. "I see you have found our Greek Road."

"Is that what it is?"

"This was the way the Greeks—who came to take over the island after the Phoenicians—traveled from the main island to Mozia. With chariots—yes?—wagons? And even in the early nineteen hundreds, farmers were driving their horse wagons on this road."

"Nineteen hundreds? It's still there?"

"Yes, yes. You can see it right under the water—"

"You know, I have seen it. I didn't know what it was then, but I saw it. Can you still travel on it now?"

"I have heard that the road is nowhere more than one meter under the water. But I am not sure—maybe we find it is broken along the way now. Who can say?"

Driving back from Marsala, Catherine pulls over at the place she and Mark had launched the kayak. She removes her left sandal to shake out a pebble. About to put it back on, she stops and removes the other instead. Somehow it's easier to walk on ground covered in pebbles than on one, however small, inside your shoe.

She sits on a large boulder and looks out over the lagoon with new eyes. The sparkling surface hides more than a playground for kayakers and the occasional windsurfer, even more than a home for fish or a refuge for birds. A road. An ancient road traveled for more than two thousand years. The lagoon holds that secret close if all you do is look. Even if you look and see the road, as she and Mark had, you haven't found it. You can't truly find something you don't know exists.

And Mozia as well, with its dusty red soil, keeps its own troubling secrets. Jaunty little jugs and scattered stone slabs, cheek by jowl with yellow, pink, and red wildflowers—that cheery scene hides a sad and dismal truth. She shivers, although the sun is hot on her skin, when she recalls Nico correcting her picture. She can't be sure his drawing is correct. It could have been childish whim that made him draw what he did. But she thinks it was more, that he knew somehow. Perhaps he lives on Mozia. His family might work in the small museum or in the vineyards. But how does he come each day to Macri? He can't walk the submerged road yet never be wet when she sees him. Even if the sun and wind could dry him, he's so small—how could he make that walk alone? It would be waist deep in places on an adult, wouldn't it? And then Catherine knows she has to try to walk the road herself.

She tucks the back hem of her wide skirt into the front of the waistband, and wading into the water until she reaches the ancient road, she steps up onto its surface, the stone so slippery with seaweed, living and dead, that she slows her already-cautious steps. She's been walking for perhaps half an hour, watching her feet the whole time, placing each foot with care. Several times, the water has reached her waist for a short period. Mostly, it has been quite shallow—thigh deep—just as it is now when she stops and looks toward Mozia. A cold hand of fear twists her stomach, and she shrinks into herself at the sheer size of the water's expanse ahead. To her left and to her right, it's more of the same. And when she turns, so slowly, and looks back at an equal stretch of water between herself and the mainland, her head throbs with horror. She's trapped—a jelly-legged speck stranded on an endless, edgeless plane. The constant southerly breeze sends a steady gentle ripple across the lagoon's surface, inducing in Catherine a dizzying sense that she's flying across the water, propelled toward Mozia by forces she can't control. She remembers times as a child, standing at the ocean's edge when large waves crashed in, first driving water shoreward, past her ankles with a great whoosh, until she would laugh with joy, sure she was moving seaward at high speed. Then the water would surge back out, sucking away the sand around her feet and creating a disorienting sense of zooming back toward land. Now, periodic swells of panic magnify her anxiety. Nauseated and immobilized, she has never felt so alone or so isolated, as if somehow someone has dropped her here and there's no going back.

Catherine covers her eyes with her hands and collects herself. It's not at all dangerous. If the water were a little deeper, she could get in and swim. She can, anytime she wants to, step off the road onto the muddy bottom, although whether that would be better or worse, she can't say. This whole thing is in her mind. Step by step is the only way. You don't look down when you're climbing—she knows that. So now, she must not look around. It's a simple matter of retracing steps already taken. It will be fine, but not if she allows herself, even for a second, to look at the deceptive scene around her, and lose her moorings in the safety of reality.

EIGHTEEN

MARK

"If it's like this in the middle of June, can you imagine August?" Mark pauses, looking up and along the path to the temple. No sign of it yet and quite a way to go. Segesta has been on their to-do list right from the start. If only they had taken the guidebook's advice and gone in April, or at least May, before it got so hot.

Catherine leans against a large rock to rest a moment before turning to continue ascending the dirt path—a series of broad, almost-level steps with worn wooden edges. No single step is a problem. There are just so many of them. Mark is going to have to get back in shape as soon as he runs out of excuses, but Catherine looks more tanned and healthy than when they arrived. She reaches the top first, and when Mark catches up, he notes the huge grin on her face before he sees anything else. Only when he looks behind her does he see the corner of the Greek Temple.

"Right?" Catherine says when he squeezes her hand. "Can you believe it?"

"This is spectacular. So—so beautifully preserved. And there's no one here."

"There'll be people later in the day, I'm sure, but right now, we kind of own this place."

"These Greek architects knew what they were doing when they picked a setting, didn't they?" On top of a high hill surrounded by lower hills of undulating green, the Temple sits in serene dominion over the surrounding farmland, much as it did almost twenty-five hundred years ago when it was new.

"So the book says seventy by one hundred eighty-five feet. One end points east. And the other west—well, yeah."

"Front to the east—typical for Greek temples." Mark approaches the building, taking in the smooth columns, the angle of the roofline, and the way the building defines its space. "Once, this was a functional building, and there were people—right here—who designed it and built it, and people who looked at it every day."

Catherine points to the west. "There's the theater out there. That's where we're going next."

"Not close, is it?"

"No." Catherine points to a shady spot. "Let's sit under those trees for a bit."

"And it's back down then *up* again, isn't it? To the theater, I mean." Mark sits on the ground.

"Yep." Catherine sits between Mark's knees, leaning on his chest. "Too hot for this? I can move."

"Worth it," says Mark.

"I love it here, Mark. This part of Sicily, I mean. I feel as if I've come home."

"It's beautiful, all right."

"It's going to be so hard leaving. I wonder if we could be happy living here."

"You serious?" Mark is used to Catherine's dreaming, but this sounds different.

"I think I am."

"I really like it here too, Cath. But I can't see us staying. I miss New York. I have a job waiting for me."

"I have a job too!" Catherine sits up and twists to face Mark. "But it's like I was born here—and before you say anything, I know that sounds silly." She sighs. "And it will be very hard to leave Nico."

"Leave Nico?" Mark wishes he hadn't sounded so incredulous.

"If you knew him, you'd feel the same way. He's so serious and lonely. He needs me."

"You've only *known* him—although to be fair, 'known' overstates it—a little over two months. He's managed his whole life before that without you. And what about me—your own husband? I wish you'd focus on the real people who need you."

Catherine stands. "*Real* people? What are you saying?"

"OK, OK. That came out wrong. And it's not even the point. But you have to admit, he's never, *ever* been around when I was. Not once. And don't you find it odd that everyone else manages to miss him too? Every time?"

"He trusts me. He isn't ready to trust you yet."

Mark stands and puts his hands on Catherine's shoulders. She pulls away. "Cath. It's been months, and no one else—"

"I know! I know that. No one has seen him but me. I don't understand it either. But there must be an explanation."

"Seriously, Cath?" He again puts his hands on her shoulders, which remain rigid under his touch, although she doesn't pull away. He softens his voice. "I sometimes wonder if you could be imagining Nico."

She shakes out from under his arms. "So you think I'm crazy?"

"I never said that. But I worry—"

"Your specialty!"

"Don't be that way." He is close to shouting. "Goddamn it, Catherine, I worry about what's going on with you."

"On with me? I—"

"Look at you! What are those ribbons in your hair?"

"They keep my hair back. That's all."

"Really? Because they look like something you'd find on a doll in a tourist stand. And that weird red vest thing with the black laces you wear sometimes, with all the embroidery and the leaves—"

Catherine's hand goes to her chest as if to cover it, although she's not wearing the vest now. "Giulia gave me that. It's hand-embroidered—all local plants and herbs."

"Well, I don't see *her* wearing anything like that. And I never saw you wear anything that—that hokey before either. But wait." He stops and holds up both hands, palms facing Catherine. "Wait. Let's not get caught up in talking about the clothes. It's not simply the clothes. It's—the thought has crossed my mind that you—maybe you're making Nico up on purpose—"

"What? Why would—"

"—but I could never come up with a reason. Until today."

"I do not understand what you are saying, Mark."

"I'm saying maybe you want to stay here, ignore everything that happened, forget your job, your colleagues—all of it. And this Nico is your excuse."

Catherine shakes her head. "I can't believe you'd say that. Any of it."

"I can't believe you've said some of the nonsense you've been saying either. Who are you anymore?"

"Because I've changed? People change, Mark. They grow."

"I don't consider an adult finding herself a five-year-old playmate—imaginary or not—to be growth."

Catherine looks away. "You know what? I'm not in the mood for the Greek theater."

"Fine. Let's just go." The only thing better would be to keep on going. Straight to the airport.

NINETEEN

CATHERINE

The next morning, Catherine walks Mark to the car in silence. They don't have much experience being angry with one another, and although she's nowhere near as furious as she was yesterday, she remains disappointed in Mark and confused. She can sense his frustration with her as well. Will two weeks apart improve the situation or allow those feelings to grow?

According to their friends, Catherine and Mark are lucky. They've grown accustomed to hearing how rare it is to see a couple who fit each other so well, who never argue, and whose mutual affection is straightforward and genuine. They've come to accept this as truth, that their life is charmed, that they are different—special. Yesterday changed all that with one brisk wallop from reality, and there's no going back or unsaying what was said. Oh, sure. They've had words before. But this was different. They'd both felt it. Worst of all, there's no denying that Mark does not feel the pull of Sicily the way she does, and he has no interest in trying to change. Which is worse—questioning her sanity or her veracity? Because he's done both.

Mark places a light kiss on Catherine's cheek. "You know how to get me."

"Have a safe trip."

"Thanks." Mark opens the car door, but turns back to Catherine. "Do you want anything from Rome? I can always pick something up if you tell me."

"Not that I can think of. But thanks."

He brushes lint she can't see from his suit jacket before hanging it inside the car and sliding into the driver's seat, one arm resting in the open window. "Well—bye, then."

"Bye." Catherine pats his arm, and the sadness in Mark's eyes deepens her own. There's no reason to think this surprising new them puzzles him any less than it does her.

TWENTY

Seth

December 22, 1992

Dear Notebook,

I made a big mistake. I sent some things to Catherine.
Just so she'd know I really wasn't some weirdo. Really
small things I thought she'd like. But if I had thought
about it more I would have known it wasn't gonna
work. They were so little and it *is* right near Christmas
and Hanukkah. In my mind when she found them
outside her office door she would be happy and think
maybe I was someone she wanted to know better. But
I think it made me look like more of a freak than
those stupid notes. God, now she probably thinks I'm
in love with her or something. Sometimes lately I feel
confused and I make really bad decisions. They seem
sensible at the time but when I look back I wonder
what the hell I was thinking. And now she ended my
extra studio time with her. She says it's her schedule
but I know it's not that. I wanted to believe that's all
it is but she still sees Karen. What if she won't let me

in her class again next semester? Or she gets someone else to teach it just to avoid me? I don't know what I'll do. I've been having those panic attacks again. I have to fix this somehow.

There's nothing good. In three days it'll be Christmas. My first one without my family. I said I'd go to my uncle's for dinner and for presents like we always all did, but I'm gonna say I'm sick or something. I'd rather stay here alone and pretend it's one more regular shitty day than be there and remember every single second that my family isn't. Karen and her boyfriend are giving a new year's eve party and she invited me. I'm not sure why, except she sees me three or four times a week in art class. Probably pity. I said I'd go but I'm gonna be sick for that too. Although I could go and make the party really special by hyperventilating in a closet the first time anyone mentions Catherine's name.

I don't sleep much. I'm up all night thinking about how the world makes no sense. Awful things keep happening. Random stuff. Yesterday, a huge plane crashed in Portugal and went on fire. 56 dead so far. A whole lot more people are in the hospital. And then today, some Libyan plane with 159 people on it "disintegrated" while it was landing in Tripoli. How can a plane disintegrate? Everybody dead of course. All these freakish accidents. Nothing makes any sense. It's hard to care much about anything when the universe is waiting to smack me down when I least expect it.

There was an earthquake someplace I never even heard of in Indonesia. An earthquake and a tidal wave and thousands of people wiped out—bam. 2500 people. I can't figure out how I'm supposed to live with all of it. Once you know that any minute some stupid thing from out of the blue could wipe you out or your family or friends—not that I have any left—but how does anything else even matter? I know that's not a "healthy" way to think, but I guess I'm not healthy yet. I can't go back to Dr W or I'll be a zombie on my daily handful of pills again. Probably even more pills than before. I really have to talk to someone. To Catherine. I know she can help me. I've got to get her to listen to me.

The Queen of England made a speech right after the fire in Windsor Castle. She called 1992 "annus horribilis"—a horrible year. I never heard that expression before, but yeah I get it. The only halfway decent thing about 92 is that it'll be gone soon. Maybe that will make some difference. I don't know. I don't know much of anything anymore.

Total dead since I started keeping track
Plane crashes: 918
Natural disasters: 5078

TWENTY-ONE

MARK

The one thing missing is Catherine. If only she could be here sharing his success. That argument they had in Segesta—if she were here, seeing what their life could be like, he's sure she would forget all about farm life in Sicily with some strange kid. The past few days, he's visited one spectacular rural property after another. His head swims with images and details that would take her mind off this country-bumpkin business. Catherine belongs with him, as a partner and as a member of the social circle he must fit into to get ahead. He's got to strengthen those connections, and Catherine—charming, intelligent, funny—is a definite asset. Or she was before this phase she's in now. Catherine has always been able to get away with an offbeat but winning personal style. He loves the way she seemed, without effort, to pull off a look that said, "I know how to be fashionable if I want to, but this is better." And there was no denying he enjoyed the cachet that accompanied having a wife who fulfilled his colleagues' expectations of an artist. What she's doing now, though—there are times she skirts around the edge of looking like an illustration on a cheap Chianti label. Imagine if she'd shown up here looking like that—like something out of the local folkloric museum.

Right now, he's at a party given by Richard and Simone Strauss. Richard, a former senior partner in the firm, took an early retirement a couple of years ago and is pursuing a second career in finance with a small, aggressive venture-capital company. From the looks of things, he's doing quite well, and Mark is more than a little in awe at being here. A lot of people talk about owning a villa, and although he's not sure what the actual definition of *villa* is, he's pretty sure this is one. And a beautiful one at that. It's the kind of place he envisions for himself and Catherine one day. Of course, they would still live most of the time in New York. But they'd be traveling here more, and Catherine's academic calendar would let them "open their villa" for the summer. Maybe something a little smaller than this would do, but certainly just as nice and with a guest bedroom or two. They could invite his parents, who'd never even been out of Wisconsin much except to visit them in New York. What a step up from that two-room cabin on the lake they went to every summer when he was growing up.

A string quartet, on an open interior balcony, plays what he thinks is Vivaldi. At the lavish buffet table filled with platters, one draws his attention. It sits next to an elegant, hand-lettered card reading "salmon and duck ceviche." Mark is helping himself to one of the delicate canapés when Simone joins him. She takes his hand and delivers a soft kiss to each of his cheeks. "Good to see you, Mark. It's been so long."

"Simone, always such a pleasure. Thank you for having me." Mark takes in Simone's chic and tasteful dress. Her hair, makeup, and jewelry are all perfection—even he sees that. In fact, the entire crowd seems to be made up of nothing but beautiful people. He feels as if someone let him in by mistake, and he might be told that the leaky sink was *that way*, and would he please attend to it at once. But next time—he'll make sure he fits in better next time.

"I understand you're a rising star now, Mark. Doing great things here. There are a few people Richard wants to make sure you meet before the evening is over."

"So I've heard. About meeting people, that is."

"No need to be modest. We're quite proud of you. And Catherine is well? After all that unfortunate business?"

"Very well, thank you. And what are you up to these days?"

"Oh, once a historian, you know. Now that we're here so much of the time, I've turned my attention to Italian culture. I'm collaborating on a paper that should be out next year. And living near Rome—well, talk about culture. It's a dream."

Mark looks for a spot to place his dish, and Simone catches the eye of a waiter at the side of the room who rushes over to relieve Mark of the plate. Simone takes Mark's arm and leads him to a pair of armchairs that whisper, "We are simple, tasteful, yet expensive." As he takes a seat, another waiter brings a tray with two heavy crystal glasses of chilled red Lambrusco and two small plates of Parmigiano-Reggiano shavings, papery-thin wafers of prosciutto, and slender strips of grilled eggplant. "Try this wine, Mark. It's lovely and dry—from Emilia-Romagna. As is everything on these plates."

Simone sips her wine. "Now tell me—where are you staying?"

"In Sicily, actually. A tiny place you probably never heard of—Macri."

The only word that comes to mind for the look on Simone's face is *astonished*. "Why there?"

"Catherine found it through a classified ad. But, Simone—that felt like more than an idle question. Was it?"

"Well, Macri is one of the more unusual Sicilian villages. On the wild and woolly side. I'm sure it's nothing more than folklore, but I envy you—staying in such a colorful place."

"Colorful . . . ?"

"It has a long history of magic, witchcraft, the evil eye—that sort of thing."

"From what I've heard, that's true of half of Sicily."

"Oh, but Macri is especially well known for familial magic." Her voice makes a subtle shift to the lecturing-professor side. "Some people call them hereditary witches, but that's not 'witch' solely as the evil sorcerer. It encompasses a more benign figure as well."

Mark finishes his Lambrusco, and a waiter appears with another. "This witch business—it probably explains the reactions I sometimes get when I tell people where we are."

"Familial magic is an ancient and secretive culture, and it exists throughout much of Italy and Sicily. Some of these families claim to trace their magic powers back five hundred years or more. Many of these villages had no doctor, so they relied on the magic powers claimed by one or more local people, usually women. It's not hard to see how believing someone can cure you with herbs or spells could lead to the belief that those same people could harm you. It's fascinating. Come." She stands and walks to a small, delicate desk in the corner of the room and hands Mark a pad and pen. He can't help thinking that the desk is probably worth more than all their furniture at home combined. "Jot down your mailing address, and I'll send you some reading you might find interesting."

As Mark writes, she says, "I don't believe in any of it, of course, but there are quite a few locals in Macri who do. They depend on their witches to heal them, solve their financial or family problems—even put the evil eye, a kind of curse, on their enemies. And people, even from outside Italy, have been known to go there, seeking help. I am jealous, Mark. It's so delicious. You might get to meet one of these magical families. And if you do, you *must* promise to tell me all about it."

TWENTY-TWO

CATHERINE

"Nico, you're my own little muse." Catherine uses her thumb to create a series of dents in the clay she's working.

Nico doesn't react. He's been here every day for the past ten days, providing just the right touch of companionship, even if it is silent. He plays with toys, sometimes with clay, and more than once has accepted a pad and pastels to draw. He draws the same thing over and over—the stone grave marker he corrected for her when she was sketching. She isn't sure if he *wants* to draw this particular thing or if it's the only thing he's ever drawn, but she's not about to rock the boat.

This morning, she arrived to find him in the studio. Sitting on her worktable was a bouquet of flowers—a motley assortment, and hand-picked, judging from the frayed and broken stems. "From you, Nico?" She had to try, even though she knew he wouldn't answer. Now, the flowers sit next to her in a vase arranged in their ragtag splendor, and more precious to Catherine than any gift has ever been.

Evidence of her recent productivity covers the closest bench. In one corner, several small statues she plans to cast in bronze appear to be in conversation with one another. She has also made a collection of sketches and, for the first time in a long time, an acrylic on canvas, an abstract inspired by the colors and textures of the lagoon.

Nico changes position, crossing his feet behind him and sitting on his heels. He studies a half-completed drawing that lies on the floor, then brings his face close to the paper and draws again. In this position, he looks like an industrious little frog, and Catherine grabs pad and pencil to sketch him. Nico makes a great subject since he remains still for long periods. Catherine has done at least a dozen sketches of Nico, but this one just begs to be a sculpture.

Mark and Catherine lie close together in bed, propped up by Giulia's large ravioli-shaped pillows, Mark's arm draped over Catherine's shoulders.

"I was a little worried that driving up so late last night would be more of a shock than a surprise."

"It was perfect. I'm glad you got home even half a day sooner. I wish you hadn't driven so many hours in one day, though."

"It was fine, but I do need my arm back." Mark sits up farther and reaches for his coffee. "It didn't feel right, being away, with you and I both so—"

"I know. Let's not do that again." She smiles. "Although you can bring us coffee in bed again anytime you want."

"Somehow here, you end up doing all the domestic stuff. We should stop that."

"I feel different here. Like I'm playing at it, almost." Catherine gets out of bed and pulls on her jeans. "I'll go make the rest of breakfast."

"Can we do it together?"

"You did your half. I'll finish, but after that I'm going to head over to the studio."

"Sounds good. I'll come over a little later this morning. I really want to see that work you said you might bring to Stefano."

"OK." A little later is good. She can use some time to clear away the sketches of Nico. No need to get into all that today. Not yet.

TWENTY-THREE

MARK

Mark had met some extraordinary people at the party, and even more at the three-day conference that followed. He'd met people from all over the globe, and few of them knew much about Sicily. The opportunities are considerable, and he wants to share it all with Catherine, the way they always used to share important things. But he'd decided to wait—to let things calm down between them first. Catherine's taking to this place the way she has—that's been a shock. Although maybe it shouldn't have been. She *is* an artist, and they practically live in an art museum here. Giulia and Assunta have gone out of their way to make her feel at home. But maybe her infatuation has peaked. She'd talked more about her work and less about Nico last night and this morning. When he gets to the studio, he hopes he'll find the old Catherine there, and they can talk, the way they used to.

"Pippo! Pippo!" Giulia's voice, coming from behind Mark, carries a note of exasperated affection. The puppy runs up to him at full speed, and Mark crouches down, causing Pippo to lick his face, threatening to devour him from sheer joy.

Giulia catches up to the jubilant puppy. "He is always ahead of me! Your big fan Pippo here—he has missed you. Was your trip a good one?"

"It was, thank you. Very good." He stands, lifting Pippo. "I'm surprised to see our little friend still here, though."

"Oh, but right now, this minute, I am taking him to the family who adopts him. He is a bug—a pest. Still, I will be sad to see him go."

"I'm sure you will."

"Only a week or two he was supposed to be here. But now, it is so long, he is like mine. Eh, what can you do?" Mark feels an unexpected pang of sadness as Giulia takes Pippo from him, and the pup wriggles and whines. "To the car, Pippo. Say good-bye to Mark now."

Mark continues toward the studio. Maybe he'll suggest a quiet little dinner in Marsala tonight. As he enters, Catherine is working in clay, looking as happy as he's ever seen her. She hasn't noticed him, so he watches in quiet. This serious side of Catherine, this intense creative side, always fills him with a sense of wonder. His work is so much more collaborative. She makes beauty from nothing and does it alone.

At the sound of her voice, he thinks at first she's talking to him and takes in a breath to say hello. But then he notices her words. "Now that I know you like puzzles, I'll get you some more. Maybe even a bigger one we can do together sometime." She pauses and stops working. "Now Mark will be here any minute, Nico, so don't run away. There's nothing to be afraid of." And there, on the edge of the shadows, a small boy sits.

Mark must have made a sound because they both look in his direction.

"Come on in. Can you see? I have a surprise for you."

He walks to Catherine. "And what is that?" He smiles.

"It's Nico! Look!" And she turns her head to the boy on the floor.

Mark looks at Nico. Nico looks straight back. Mark meets the boy's solemn eyes, then turns to Catherine.

"Where?"

The joy on Catherine's face falls away, and she searches Mark's face for a sign, he supposes, of something she can make sense of. "But—you were looking right at him. Right there!" She turns and points to Nico's spot on the floor. All that remains is a pile of toys.

"Near those toys? Is he in the dark there? I can't—" He moves his head back and forth, scanning.

Catherine sits. "I do not understand."

"I guess he left suddenly again?"

"No, Mark. You were looking right at him. I saw you looking right there. How—?" She rubs her forehead with her fingertips.

"What are you saying?"

"I'm saying that you and I were both looking straight at Nico." She looks up into Mark's face, her eyes filled with fear. "But only I saw him."

Mark wipes a thin film of perspiration from his upper lip. He's not sure what's more terrifying—his sudden decision to lie to her, or his equally sudden realization of what the fallout from this is going to be. "It had to have been a trick of the light, Cath. Something like that."

"No. No. That can't explain this. It can't."

Mark sits next to her. "Catherine. There has to be—"

"Something is terribly wrong, Mark. What's happening? What's happening to me?"

"How does he do that without burning himself?" At their favorite restaurant in Marsala, Mark and Catherine sit at an outdoor table. They have a clear view of the fire juggler tonight. He's here every weekend, a gangly young man who arrives right after dusk. He always lays a small blanket on the cobblestoned street where he places a collection bowl, a cassette player, and a black rectangular case containing—well—whatever fire jugglers need, Mark supposes. He hopes a first-aid kit is in there.

Catherine, appearing groggy and distracted, doesn't reply, so Mark tries again. "The learning curve must be interesting." He takes a sip of wine and waits. She picks at her food like a child in a spinach patch.

"Is that a new necklace you're wearing?" Mark doesn't recognize it. Bright red, lustrous, and shaped like a tiny tree, it reminds Mark of something.

Catherine brings her hand to it. "Giulia gave it to me today. It's coral. Supposed to bring good luck." She continues to push her food around on the plate.

"Don't like your salad?"

She puts down the large silver fork. "It's fine. I'm not hungry. Not after today."

"We do need to talk about it, Cath."

"*It*. Yes. I suppose we do. It's all I can think about."

Mark takes Catherine's hand in both of his. "Catherine, honey." He ducks his head and looks up into her eyes. "Look at you."

"What can I say, Mark?"

"I just want you to know I'm worried."

"Because I'm imagining things."

"You've been through a lot. I think maybe what happened back home—maybe it had a bigger effect on you than either of us realized."

Catherine takes her hand back and wraps her arms around her shoulders. "I wish I'd brought a sweater."

"This whole Nico thing, this attachment you feel to a place you've never even been before, the way you're dressing now when you're not in your work jeans—"

"Not that again, Mark. It's all local. Giulia helps me pick things out."

"That's interesting, but I kind of miss the more sophisticated side of you." An image flashes into his mind of the people at Richard and

Simone's party. "It feels like part of an effort to lose yourself here. The whole thing does."

"The whole *thing*? It's a *thing*?" Catherine watches the juggler until he stops for a break. "Maybe it is. Right now, I can't even tell."

Mark recognizes this as his moment. "Listen, you need to get away from here. For a breather. A short one. Come with me next week to Riposto. We'll spend a few days relaxing. Having fun. You'll love it there. We need to do something because I'm getting concerned about you."

"I'm more than a little concerned about myself right now too." Picking up her fork, Catherine pokes at her food again. "Maybe you're right. But are you sure this is a good time for me to go with you?"

"Couldn't be better. I have a few local places to visit this week, and then I can go."

"I do need to visit Stefano in Florence. If I can arrange that for after Riposto, do you want to continue on? Come with me?"

"Sure. Who doesn't want to go to Florence?" Mark taps Catherine's fork, which is still in her hand. "Now would you eat something, please?" He smiles. "Everything is going to be fine. You'll see."

The anguish behind Catherine's weak smile shames Mark. "I hope you're right."

"I am. Trust me." He's gotten what he wanted. Why does he feel so empty?

TWENTY-FOUR

CATHERINE

With her visit to Stefano arranged, Catherine now works on more material to bring along. She's looking right at Nico, playing here in the studio, as clearly as she looks at anyone else. Yesterday's events feel like one more bad dream. There must have been a misunderstanding. Mark might not have been looking where she thought he was. And then Nico had left, and that confused both of them. There's no other reasonable explanation. When Mark comes in today, he'll meet Nico, and they'll laugh together about the whole thing over dinner tonight.

"I'm getting ready to leave!" Mark's voice carries from outside the studio.

"Well, come on in and say good-bye, then." As she hops down from her stool, she glances to Nico, who shows no sign of having heard Mark.

Mark approaches Catherine. "I'll be back by dinnertime, OK? I have to run."

"Mark, wait! Look." She points to Nico on the floor. Nico does not look up.

"Cath—You don't—Are you saying he's here?" Mark moves his head from side to side as if trying to see around an obstacle.

Catherine shrinks into herself as if a weight pushes her down, and she grasps the back of her stool. Wanting to scream, all she can do is whisper. "You don't see him?"

"I wish I did." Mark's face conveys bewildered concern. He pushes a loose strand of hair behind her ear. "Look. I'm late. But I'm worried about leaving you. Let me go call and cancel my meeting."

"That's not necessary."

"But you . . ."

"Please just go. I'm fine." She sits on her stool, arranging her tools on the table. A hazy film—a dried slurry of spilled water and clay—camouflages the dark wood surface. Snaking edges lend the film a look of a gossamer cloth carelessly tossed. The same film cloaks the rosewood handle of the tools, turning them ghostly gray, and from the proper angle, they blend into the table. By moving her head, she can make the tools nearly disappear.

"Promise me you'll call Giulia if you don't feel right?"

"I'm OK. I'll see you at dinner."

"If you're sure—"

"I'm sure. I'll be fine."

Catherine watches Mark leave the barn, listens to his car door slam and his tires crunch as the car fades down the driveway. Her hands are too shaky to work the clay now, but that's no longer her first order of business. Nico sits unmoved and unchanged, playing as if nothing has happened. He did not run away from Mark, did not even react to Mark's arrival. What does any of this mean?

Picking up a sketch pad, Catherine doodles in what she hopes is a casual manner. "Nico, did you see Mark come in?"

He looks at her. She thinks she detects a smile—an unpleasant smile, in his eyes only—but she's not sure.

"I think maybe you did. I wish I understood what was going on."

Catherine flips the page. "I'm going to come sit on the floor with you, OK? Because I can see you better, and I want to draw that cute face. Yes?" She sits down cross-legged, facing Nico, about six feet in front of him. He scrambles to change position so that he sits cross-legged as well. Catherine smiles, and Nico meets her gaze as she holds out a pad and pencil to him. "Let's draw."

As Catherine sketches, her shaking subsides. Whatever is going on, there is an explanation. "Nico, you never told me—do you have a mother and father?"

He keeps sketching.

"Brothers and sisters?"

No reaction.

She draws awhile, then pauses. "Where do you go to school? Or preschool?" He doesn't even look up. "I bet you live in a nice place. Is it close to here?" He nods—one clipped downward dip of his chin. Something! But was that yes to it being nice or close by? Or was it a yes at all? Catherine tries to learn more, but Nico grows wary, and she wants him to stay.

"I have an idea. Why don't you draw a picture for me? Of yourself. Of—how about of where you were last night? And I'll draw one for you—of me where I was last night. OK?" He meets her gaze with no change in expression and starts to draw. Catherine does the same. She sketches the restaurant table in Marsala, the casual strollers in the streets, and the fire juggler in the act of crouching to catch a flaming torch.

It's more and more clear that there are only two possibilities: either Mark cannot see Nico and she can, or she has lost her mind. Perhaps you can't tell when you lose contact with reality, but surely, other things would be out of whack as well. And it can't be Mark—levelheaded, practical Mark. So what's left? Can Nico be a ghost? She doesn't even believe in that kind of thing. There must be something she's not thinking of.

"Catherine? Catherine?" It's Giulia.

Catherine gets up from the floor and brushes the dirt from the seat of her jeans. "I'll be right back, Nico. Wait, OK?"

Giulia comes in carrying a tray with a teapot and a plate covered in a cloth napkin.

"Giulia! Here, let me get that. Did you carry it all the way here?"

"Of course! I grew up working the land. I have muscles."

Catherine inspects the tray as she carries it over to a bench. "Tea? I love it, but I didn't think you did. Just a few days ago you said coffee was for healthy people and tea for the sick." She laughs.

"Well, Mark says to me today that perhaps you are not so well, and so I come to look in on you."

"Oh." She feels betrayed.

"This is a special herb tea I made for us. To help you feel better."

"I see. Well, that's very nice of you. Now——" But an intuition comes over Catherine, and before she looks, she knows deep in her bones that Nico is gone. At his spot, she picks up his pad. He has made a drawing, childish but clear, of a boy. The boy has hair like Nico's and wears a striped shirt with shorts. He lies flat on his back, eyes closed. He could be sleeping or—her stomach lurches and she shivers—he could be dead.

"Yes?" Giulia has come over to Catherine, who closes the pad.

"It's nothing. Let's have our tea. What's under the cloth?"

"Cookies. Like we made together. Bones of the Dead."

Catherine sits in one of Giulia's comfortable lounge chairs facing the lagoon. All she can think about is Nico's picture; she never managed to get back to work after Giulia left. She'd love to follow Nico, to see where he goes, but she has no idea how. She can't very well grab him or put him on a leash and insist he take her along. She can't even get very close to him most of the time. Any move to force the issue could break his trust in her. He might never come back.

She's come here to read about Mozia, and the book she bought in Marsala lies closed in her lap now, her finger marking her place. It's hardly an academic text, but it's filling in some blanks, including a disquieting theory about the children's cemetery. Evidence suggests—and this brings back dim memories from freshman art history—it was no ordinary cemetery. She must have walked right by the most damning sign without recognizing it—the adjacent tophet. Found in many Phoenician settlements, tophets were places the faithful offered sacrifices to the King of the Gods, Ba'al-Hammon. The most horrible part is that they would sacrifice not only animals but—unspeakably—their own small children, often the firstborn. To think that she sat among the remains of those tormented children, victims "consigned to the fire" to ensure a good harvest or favorable weather—it was beyond hideous. What she'd foolishly thought she'd "discovered"—a private, windswept refuge—was in fact a bleak, desolate unholy ground, the time-scattered ashes and tiny bone fragments of betrayed children underfoot, trampled like so much dirt.

It sickens her to think it, but this could be Nico's story, the reason he was familiar with the stele she was drawing. As much as she dances around the bigger questions it raises, the idea that Nico is a ghost has been insistent, forcing its way into her thoughts for a while now. She's resisted it, as anyone would. Ideas you can't explain, even to yourself—that you can't envision trying to explain to anyone else without the worst kind of embarrassment—these ideas beg for dismissal. But now, she can't think of a better reason for a "spirit" to be restless than this. And Nico's own drawing—that mournful, chilling drawing—it would make sense. Nico as a ghost would explain so many things. And Nico as this particular ghost would explain his deep distrust of people and his urge to run. What it wouldn't explain is why he has chosen Catherine.

TWENTY-FIVE

SETH

January 29, 1993

Dear Notebook,

You're the only one who listens to me anymore. At least I think you listen. I failed totally with Catherine. I made matters worse. I tried to explain myself by writing letters. I got really nice paper. Beautiful paper I thought she would really like. And she would see that I was serious and that these were serious letters, not some love notes from some kid. I think she read them. She answered the first 2 but with really short answers so I don't know if she read them all the way through even. I feel like such an idiot I can't even go to her class anymore. The one person who paid any attention to me at all and that I felt a connection to and now she probably wishes she had never heard my name. Not taking that class messes up when I can graduate but I don't care anymore. She even suggested I go to a shrink. Suggested AGAIN, because she said that before when I did all those fire paintings. I guess she could tell something was wrong. See, that's why I need to talk to her. She knows me. But I guess I have to give that up and try to get my act together.

I think I may have to go back to Dr W. All this not sleeping is making me feel weird. A few times lately I saw some guy I don't know just looking at me on campus. And yesterday he was walking down the street right outside this apartment when I got home. Why would anyone want to follow me? It's nuts. I'm nuts. All I want is to live my life with no meds and no "assignments" about visualizing things and biofeedback and writing about my thoughts for HIM to read. I feel frozen. I guess I have to try to work up the courage to call him up and go back.

Next month it will be a year since the fire. Exactly one month from today. That blows my mind. There's no way I can get through that without some help. So, yeah, that's my job now. I have to work up the courage and try to call him. Soon. Even if going back is one more miserable failure.

PS If you're keeping track, Notebook, another plane crash in the Congo killed 12 people 2 days ago. And one in Paris killed 4. Plus a ferry sank in Turkey and 52 people got killed. It's everywhere you look.

Total since I started keeping track
Plane crashes: 934
Natural disasters: 5078
Other disasters: 52

TWENTY-SIX

MARK

In the Palermo office, Mark takes his mail from Paola, thanks her, and heads off to the empty conference room that serves as his workspace when he visits. As he sorts through notes from potential clients, contract drafts from lawyers, and other work-related materials, he finds a fat envelope from Simone containing a packet of photocopied pages. Clipped to the outside is a note on stationery embossed with her initials: "Following up on our conversation with some reading I think you'll enjoy. It was lovely seeing you the other night. Don't be a stranger. And next time, please do bring Catherine."

Half an hour later, Mark is pretty well steeped in the history of Macri and its deep connection to magic. He'll have to remember to ask Giulia about it one day. It could definitely earn him some points with Simone, and that would probably knock on to Robert and his connections. Can't hurt.

Much of the information she sent revolves around benign or even positive things—healing the sick, helping to arrange a happy marriage, and bringing blessings upon a family with a new baby. But there is some pretty disturbing stuff in here as well: dolls with pins in them, evil spells, shape-shifting, dream visits. And it runs the range from protracted petty spats to serious harm inflicted on another—destroying family harmony, ruining crops, sickening and killing people. There are even reports of killing and eating infants. Stranger still, women who can transform themselves into birds or wolves and travel around at night, seeking out their enemies and paralyzing them in their beds. None of it seems as if it could possibly be going on around the Macri he's seen.

However, Mark recognizes from his reading the charm he has seen some people—men, women, and children—wear around their necks. A hand with only the pointer and pinkie fingers extended and aimed downward, the *corna* is thought to have magic powers, as are certain herbs, branches, and even coral. It's all very colorful, all right. A bunch of nonsense but colorful as hell.

◆　◆　◆

Mark returns after dark, the yellow glow from the cottage the only thing lighting his way to the door. He studies Catherine through the windows. What a relief not to find her asleep on the couch or looking sad and puzzled, the way she'd been when he left today. In fact, she looks happy, working in the kitchen, surrounded by food.

"I knocked off work early and made dinner for us."

"I see." Mark takes in the chaos in the kitchen.

"I know—me cook, right? Go ahead and laugh. But I thought it would be nice for a change." She smiles. "So how did it go today?"

"Good." He gives Catherine a quick hello kiss. Things are looking up. With Catherine feeling this much better already, a short break from here should have her back to her old self in no time.

"What can I do?"

"Nothing yet. I am—and it's a miracle—approaching self-sufficient in the kitchen, thanks to Giulia and Assunta. You know, I rarely eat out anymore when you're not here." Catherine shakes the water from a large bunch of fresh basil. "Tonight we're having three of their favorite recipes, which, let's see . . ." She consults some food-stained notes on the counter. "Reduce heat, cook four or five minutes more . . . OK! Which should be ready any minute."

Mark reaches for the lid of a heavy pottery dish, but Catherine grabs his hand. "Wait! That's just out of the oven." She hands him an oven mitt in a purple-and-green grapevine design.

He lifts the lid. "And this is?"

"*Involtini di melanzane.*"

"Which old Mark would have thought had to do with electrified melons or something, but more worldly Euro-Mark knows means rolled-up eggplant with the magic of deliciousness."

"I hope you're right about the deliciousness. And this is *frocia ai carciofi* in the pan."

"Mmmm. That little miracle of artichokes and eggs."

"I made a green salad, and for dessert we have cookies that Giulia brought by this afternoon."

"That was nice of her."

"I know you asked her, Mark. It's OK." Her voice is light. She looks around the kitchen counter. "Notice anything different on the walls?"

Mark looks and notices three ornate frames. "What are those?" He walks over to examine them.

"Pressed herbs. Giulia showed me how to make them today. They're a traditional decoration. Three in here, three in the bedroom. My favorite is the one that's all branched. It's rue, which Giulia said is the herb of regret. Kind of poetic, isn't it?"

"A little weird, really." And since when was Catherine into arts and crafts? Isn't this the kind of thing she would have been merciless in skewering a few short months ago?

"You think they're weird? I think they're sweet and sort of folksy. Speaking of herbs, where's that basil? And can you open the wine?"

Mark finds the intricate corkscrew in one of the cluttered drawers and applies it to the bottle with caution. It might be easier to open the wine with his teeth than with this Byzantine metal contraption, but he manages at last.

Catherine hums, finishing up last details. "I figured something out today."

"What's that?"

"Well"—she pauses and looks at Mark—"first let's get everything out on the table."

Mark gasps. She knows he lied. How? And why isn't she angry?

"You can start with bringing the wine over there." She meant food. On the actual table. Not the confession his guilty conscience had assumed.

Catherine has put a white embroidered cloth on the table, and now she touches a match to a pair of pale-gray candles and turns out the lights. "Pretty?"

"Very." He thinks he sounds calm, but it will be a few minutes before his heart settles down. "Before we begin—" Mark lifts his wineglass. "To us."

Catherine taps her glass on Mark's, and they drink, Mark draining his glass in a single shot. The food is surprisingly good, although he suspects more diplomatic wording would be wise. He's about to make a stab at it when Catherine speaks.

"So. You ready?" She puts her fork down, folds her hands in her lap, and sits up straight, a fourth grader preparing to recite her first poem for her grandparents.

"Shoot."

"I figured out what's going on with you and Nico."

Mark slows his chewing, his mouth so dry he's unsure he can swallow.

"A lot of things I've always thought were nonsense—old wives' tales, whatever—turn out to be true when you look into them. Even if they sound crazy. And well, anyway—" She takes a deep breath. "I'm pretty sure Nico is a ghost."

Mark looks at Catherine, waiting for her to say "Gotcha!" but he can tell from her eyes that she's serious. She means it. It was inevitable. There was no way he could have said what he did without consequence, no matter how hard he tried to close his eyes to that fact, to hope he'd be able to finesse it. But how? What else has his stupid behavior, his inane lie, left her to conclude? That one of them is crazy? That he's lying? That's what hurts the most—she probably never considered the latter.

"Are you serious, Cath? Because that's pretty *out there*." He pours more wine for both of them, spilling some in the process. He watches the purple stain bleed into the tablecloth. Catherine quickly dips a finger into the small puddle and dabs some wine behind Mark's ear, then her own. "Assunta told me that spilling wine is bad luck—unless you do that." Mark jumps up for a dish towel, grateful for something to do, for an opportunity to hide the guilt he's sure is plain on his face.

"I know it's out there, but yes, I'm serious." And she tells him about the cemetery, the tophet, and the ritual child sacrifice. "So you see, it would all make sense if Nico is one of those children."

"Sense. Well—Cath, I don't know what to say."

"Look, I know you worry about me, but don't. I'm not afraid in the least. It's actually kind of, well—kind of wonderful." She doesn't seem to notice Mark's silence. "I never believed in ghosts. I mean, in books and movies about them, it's always *a haunting*." She raises her hands into the air and waves her fingers. "All woo-woo and scary and dark. Terrifying. I thought if I ever did see a ghost, or think I saw one, I would freak out completely. But that's not the way it is. This is—I don't know—kind of thrilling. He picked me! And he doesn't want to hurt me or drink my blood or any other nonsense. He's a sad little boy who wants someone to care about him. And I do. I care."

Mark fears that speaking will telegraph his terrible shame. The thought of eating nauseates him. He can't bear to look at Catherine's glowing face and know that he and only he is responsible for her delusions.

"Aren't you going to say anything, Mark?"

That puzzled look, that trusting, puzzled look on Catherine's face—he can't get past that, can't think of what to say.

"Wait. Don't. It's OK. I can imagine how it sounds. I know how it would sound to me, or would have before this. Just think about it for a while. Let it sink in."

"Fine." Mark grabs the safety line she's thrown and nods. "Fine. We'll talk about it tomorrow."

"Aren't you gone tomorrow?"

"Oh, right. In the day. How about you meet me for dinner in Marsala and we'll talk then?" And her open shining face, her total outright joy, nearly kills him.

At an outdoor table of what they now think of as "their little restaurant," Mark leans back in his seat and stretches. The thought that any minute Catherine will bring up the subject of Nico has him all but jumping out of his skin.

"The street's crowded tonight, isn't it?" Mark tries for a short delay of the inevitable.

A group of laughing young people stroll by, one member walking backward, facing the others, and singing a song whose melody is familiar. The others laugh and comment, presumably on his singing technique.

"Isn't that the big Whitney Houston hit? The one where she always sounds like she sat on a tack?"

Catherine listens. "Yup. 'I Will Always Love You.' From that movie you hated. *The Bodyguard.*"

"Right. You mean 'Eye-eeeeeee-eye Will Always Love *Yoooo-ooo-ooo-ooo-ooouuu.*'"

Laughing, Catherine says, "You're such a grouch about things like that."

"Things like yodeling, you mean?"

"Well, I like it." The group is no longer in earshot, and after a pause, Catherine says, "So. Have you had a chance to think about what I told you last night?"

"Actually, it was hard to get it out of my mind."

"And?"

He sighs. "And—I don't know—" He sounds whiny, pleading. He hears it. "Cath, look at this night. Let's not waste it talking about that right now. Your little ghost isn't going anywhere and—"

"Waste? My little ghost?" Catherine looks around at the other diners, then back to Mark. "Sorry. I don't mean to be so loud, but that's pretty damn offensive."

"Come on. You can't really believe all that stuff. It's a fun idea and all, and you're a very creative person. But—"

"So, you're saying I invented this whole ghost idea why? To entertain myself?"

"I didn't say that. And I didn't *mean* that. But you do have a great imagination."

"And inventing a ghost beats facing the fact that I have daily hallucinations. *That's* what you're saying."

"Where did you—? No! I didn't say that either. But you can't forget what you went through last semester."

"Meaning?"

"Meaning isn't there something a little coincidental about finding another boy who needs you?"

"This is not going well. Not at all."

"Let's back up. Let me finish my original thought. I think we should postpone talking about it until after we get back from Riposto, because my honest belief is that you're kind of delicate right now, and once you're away from this environment, things will look different to you."

Catherine stares at the arm of her chair. Her voice is soft, defeated. "Delicate. That feels like a nice word for *psycho*."

"It isn't. Please, you have to trust me about this."

"How? Let's say we go away and I realize Nico is a figment of my imagination. That I never saw him. Do you think I can just say"—she leans back in her seat, hands on hips—"'Well, that was different!' and go on as if nothing is wrong?"

"I think you'll see that you've been caught up in a story land here, one that appeals to the artist in you so much that your mind is playing tricks on you." And after two weeks, with any luck, the kid will give up and never come back.

"I don't know. I hear what you're saying, but I still believe Nico is a ghost. Not some kind of compensating fantasy for my past mistakes."

"See what I mean? Let's not talk about it anymore right now. Let's not build sides. We're on the same side, aren't we?" Mark squirms from the hypocrisy of his own words. He's built the sides with his ill-considered lie. Ill-considered? Not considered at all. What did he think she was going to do—shrug it all off? Had he not spoken on impulse, had he not led with his emotions, they wouldn't be in this situation.

Catherine sighs. "All right. I won't say any more. Right now."

"Tomorrow, we'll just enjoy ourselves in Erice. And the next day, we'll be off to Riposto. It's gonna be great. You'll see."

"I'm going to run into the ladies'. I'll be out in a minute."

Mark watches Catherine enter the restaurant, and when her scarf slips from her shoulders and she stoops to pick it up, she appears so vulnerable in his eyes that the guilt is overwhelming. He looks away, looks across the back of Catherine's empty chair and down the street. His stomach heaves and his breath tightens as he finds himself looking straight at Nico, not more than twenty yards away. The fire juggler is between them, and Nico's face appears, stony cold, in intermittent flashes between the hot flames of the tossed clubs. Nico holds Mark's gaze for five, maybe six seconds, then turns away and fades into the crowd. Mark finishes his wine, pours himself what remains from the bottle, and signals the waitress for another.

◆ ◆ ◆

Craggy, medieval Erice, set on a mountaintop, was veiled in a gossamer mist earlier today. But the sun has done its job, and the town that guidebooks struggle to describe—there are, after all, only so many words for *beautiful*—now displays itself to perfection. The road up had been all hairpin turns and magical views of mountains and ocean and of the town itself above. Now, walking through the town, Mark has lost count of how many rolls of film he's shot. With fortresses, castles, and turrets everywhere, he can't stop snapping. Maybe Catherine had been right about borrowing one of those new digital cameras for this trip. And he might have agreed, but who wanted to be responsible for such an expensive item? And the technology—he doesn't quite trust it. How is a picture you can't hold in your hand even real?

Catherine had waited to pull out her sketch pad until they were deep into some of the winding, hilly streets where she couldn't resist the wood and stone embellishments of the buildings and doorways that surrounded her. It was the variety of niches, each with a petite statue of the Madonna, and each eccentric and winning in its own way, that she drew with a concentration he recognized. Some of these would surely show up in her work.

Right now, Catherine draws a pink-cheeked Madonna, one with a golden crown and a milky vase of fresh red flowers at her side. Mark takes the opportunity to explore the nearby side streets. Each street here is unique, and although all are stone, some are long, narrow, and curving with a steep slope, and others are terraced into broad, shallow steps. None are flat; none are straight. Buildings in all shades of brown and pink step right up to the edge of the road, meeting the jumble of pedestrians and cars without benefit of sidewalks or buffers of any kind.

Nooks, crannies, and impossibly small alleyways abound, some going off at odd and rash angles, mysterious off-ramps, to where is unclear. Here and there, stone archways straddle the street, framing the view beyond. The effect is a glorious multidimensional maze through space and time.

As he walks, Mark keeps count of his turns so he can find his way back to Catherine. On a deserted side street, as he studies an arch, running his hand over the stone, a scuffling sound draws his attention. He looks up in time to see Nico and makes the briefest eye contact before the child disappears around a corner. Third time today.

Shaken, Mark turns and retraces his steps to Catherine, who stands holding a map. Keeping one finger anchored on the map, she keeps turning to the left and right in what looks like an attempt to orient herself to her confusing surroundings. He feels a stab of irritation. Why not just turn the map?

She looks up as he approaches. "Oh, good. You found me. These streets are like sets of concentric triangles, if that's even a thing. I'm not sure where we are. Or how we ever got here."

Mark looks at the map over Catherine's shoulder. "I think that's the restaurant Giulia recommended," he says, pointing down a crowded side street.

She looks up. "You OK? You sound funny."

"Just hungry."

Catherine, squinting, points to a gray building in the distance. "That? With the black sign?"

He points again. "No. I meant the one next to . . ." Mark's heart pounds and he drops his arm. Nico stands in front of the restaurant. "Cath, do you see what I see?" Mark keeps his eyes on Nico, who turns and walks away.

"What?"

"Nothing. For a minute I thought I saw someone I knew."

TWENTY-SEVEN

SETH

February 22, 1993

Dear Notebook,

Yesterday might have been the worst day in my life not counting the fire of course. I got called before a disciplinary council at school. Catherine was there and her husband and me. I was already totally freaked out about having to be there but then I saw her husband and I thought oh God, I recognize him and they're saying I harassed them—both of them—and could it be possible that I did? Because why would I know him at all? But then no, I knew. It isn't possible. I would remember if I followed someone around. I know I would. But then I almost passed out because I thought he might be the guy I saw looking at me on the street a few times. I couldn't even concentrate on what they were saying for a while because it was making me sick—all these wild thoughts running through my head. I can't see why he would do that so all I could think was I must be delusional. But then I thought, no, lots of guys look like him and I never got a really good look, so I'm OK. I'm OK. And I calmed down some, but I must have been sweating and looking pretty guilty.

Catherine never even looked at me much, and when she did, I saw pity on her face. She talked about the notes and letters and presents. She didn't really want to. I could see that. Her husband, though—he said I was stalking him. He named all these places I hung out looking for him. And watched him in some creepy way. Oh God, Notebook. Maybe it happened. Maybe when I thought someone was watching me it was because I was watching him? But NO. No. That can't be. I didn't even know where he worked before he said it at the meeting. I know now, though, and I've never been anywhere near there. When it was my turn, I told them all that. Not about him watching me. I was afraid they'd have me committed or something. But I couldn't prove I wasn't where he said I was. I have no friends and I'm always here alone. Too bad you can't talk, Notebook. You would have vouched for me. So I got asked to take a semester off. Yeah—asked. Ha. And told I had to leave Catherine and her husband alone. It's like a restraining order, only the school issues it. And if I don't obey it, I think maybe they can take me to court and get a real one.

I can't figure out why her husband is making this stuff up about me. Because he has to be making it up. Maybe he saw that *Bodyguard* movie. Everyone was talking about it a couple of months ago. Maybe that gave him ideas about a stalker? I don't know. Maybe Catherine complained about me to him and he's trying to fix it up. I hate myself when I think I might have upset her that much. She's so nice and never did a thing to me. I never meant to do anything to her either. What a fucking mess.

The catastrophes in the papers were worse this time than usual even. There was a midair collision in Iran and 133 people died. Even those words "midair collision" terrify me. Like the word fuselage. It's a horrible word. You never ever hear it or read it except when there's a plane crash. I can't even sleep sometimes thinking about those words. Midair collision. Like you're up there. You're sitting out there in the air. And it must be really loud when it happens. Maybe some of them saw the other plane coming. I don't know. It must have been really fast. And horrible. There must have been so much fire. Like the department store in China that went on fire and 79 people got killed. And another ferry sank. In Haiti and they don't even know how many people died. Like 1500 or even more. How come it's always such a round number? Are people so cheap in this world we don't even have to count them exactly? What's so strange is that the exact same day a ferry in Denmark almost sank but they saved everybody. So sometimes it works out. Like that Lufthansa plane that got hijacked last week but no one got killed. No doubt about it. The laughing clown picks some of us to be the lucky ones.

I've got to call Dr W this week. I need someone's help and if I have to take some pills for a while, well, at least I have no classes or anything to go to. I have nothing to get in my way. Because I have nothing at all.

Total dead since I started keeping track

Plane crashes: 1067

Natural disasters: 5078

Other disasters: 1631

TWENTY-EIGHT

MARK

As Mark had suspected and hoped, Catherine has fallen head over heels for Roberto's place in Riposto. And who wouldn't? Opening that big gate and driving along the private road lined with palm trees and through the rolling groves of lemon, you can't help but give in to the scent of citrus and jasmine. At the end of the drive, a broad expanse of lawn waits with open arms. The old stone farmhouse claims pride of place there until the eye roams to spectacular views of the Ionian Sea in one direction and Mount Etna, a cap of smoke and clouds atop its peak, in the other. Roberto and his mother are warm and welcoming hosts, and the rooms are comfortable and homey. The children are not around much, which, right now, is fine with Mark. He has a vision of this spectacular property becoming an *agriturismo* with small outbuildings matching, as well as can be managed, the main house in style and character, able to accommodate many more visitors than their current two extra rooms permit.

He and Catherine have fallen into an easy pattern of breakfast on the patio, days poking around tiny villages, and evenings playing cards and sitting outside in the warm darkness watching Mount Etna put on a show. There's a small eruption going on, and although the locals take little to no notice, Mark and Catherine can't get enough of the mountain's bewitching transition from daytime blue through shades of gray against an orange-streaked sky until, as the sun tucks itself behind the mountain, Etna blends into the black, leaving behind a Cheshire-cat grin of red lava glowing in the night. Some evenings, they've been lucky enough to catch sight of a lava plume shooting upward, a silent flash of a glowing red phantom in the placid night sky.

Today, they've driven up to Etna. Roberto had warned them they could drive only about halfway up the mountain, showing them on a map where they must park. Since there was an eruption, they would have to abide by the signs and barriers in place for their safety.

Parking the car, Mark sets the emergency brake. "Looks like a great place to hike around. I wonder what Roberto's mother sent in that basket. I feel like a little kid. I haven't had someone pack lunch for me since fifth grade."

They arrange a blanket on the ground and sit. "Some hikers we are! Right back on our keisters." Catherine laughs. "Come on. Let me take your picture over there, with the top of Etna behind you and the light so pretty. OK?"

Mark walks until Catherine says to stop, then turns and poses, the smoking crater behind him in the distance.

"Stop frowning!" Catherine adjusts the camera settings and frames the photo. "We want to believe you're happy to be here."

"I'll try, but I'm looking into the sun."

"Well, then turn your head a little bit."

As Mark turns away from the direct sunlight, his relaxed happiness gives way to alarm. He squints. It can't be! Off to the side, behind Catherine, Nico watches. How could he possibly have gotten here? Did he stow away in the trunk? Is it coincidence—he just happened to be here today? Mark's head feels at least twice its normal size, all spongy and too heavy for his neck. Sweat beads on his forehead, and a growing nausea makes it harder and harder to hide his unease. "I need to sit down a minute."

"You all right?" Catherine slings the camera strap over her shoulder and holds Mark's arm as they go back to their blanket.

"I'm fine."

"You sure? You've been acting funny lately."

"It's nothing." But "nothing" can't make you feel like this. "Nothing" can't track you down wherever you are.

It's their fourth day in Florence, and as far as Mark can tell, things couldn't be better with Catherine and Stefano. They've worked together daily until early afternoon, and Mark has enjoyed his time here alone. With Catherine's tips for avoiding the worst of the crowds, he's managed several times to be the only visitor to some little off-the-beaten-track church or museum. The best part is he hasn't seen Nico—except for possibly one time, but he wasn't certain it was Nico at all. The more he thinks about it, the surer he is that he overreacted to a random child who looked his way.

Yesterday, Stefano had received the go-ahead to show Catherine the statue he wants her to work on. Mark's not sure he understands Catherine's explanation: a growing demand for bronze copies of antique works requires copies to be exquisitely faithful to the original. This entails a meticulous multistage process and specialized skills—skills Catherine learned from Stefano years ago. Museums can lend out the copies of their most valuable works for display and study. In some places, to protect irreplaceable items from accidental or deliberate damage by members of the public, museums even display copies themselves, keeping the original in safe storage.

Catherine has asked Mark to meet her at two p.m. at the Uffizi—one of the most important museums in the world—so he can see the statue when she does. Now, he checks his watch and steps up his pace. It might not matter to anyone else around here, but he likes to be on time. As he nears the Uffizi, Mark keeps an eye out for Catherine and waves when he catches sight of her.

"Come on," she says. "We get to go in a private entrance!" Catherine approaches a guard and shows him a laminated ID card.

"I'm so excited, I could explode. Stefano told me what the statue is. They have it in a private room for us."

"Would I know it?"

"It isn't the *Pietà* or anything, if that's what you mean. It's called the *Spinario*. That means 'thorn picker.' But people call it *Boy with Thorn*. It's an incredible Roman bronze. A beautiful one. I saw it when I was here the first time. Right now it's on loan to the Uffizi from a conservatory in Rome. And they've given permission for us to make and keep a single copy." Mark notices the "us," a good sign. "Obviously, I'd have to work on it here, but I wouldn't have to be here all the time by any means."

Catherine's pace grows quicker as her excitement escalates, and Mark has trouble keeping up. She stops and takes a deep breath when she reaches a large door set into a marble frame at the end of the corridor.

"You sure I belong?" Mark already feels like a fifth wheel.

"Of course. This is a real privilege, seeing something like this with no ropes, no crowds, nothing. I want you to see it too." She presses a buzzer set discreetly into the wall, and a guard lets them in.

Soft natural light pours in through six tall windows on the outer wall and through multiple skylights in the double-height ceiling. In the center of the room is the statue. Larger than life-size, it depicts a seated young boy with one foot bare and upturned on the opposite knee. His face is a study in concentration as he tries to remove a thorn from the foot. Stefano is there, as are another man and a woman, both impeccably dressed and representing the Uffizi. Catherine makes introductions.

"So, Catherine—and of course Mark," says Stefano. "Look as much as you like." The expression on Stefano's face suggests a man about to hand out cigars.

"A small human moment—so common, so unimportant—captured thousands of years ago." Catherine touches the boy's hair. "A little change in the haircut and it could be today."

"Yes," says Stefano. "And perhaps my favorite thing about it is that we also call it *Fedele*—" He turns to Mark. "This means faithful. Because some think this is a messenger boy who completed his task, making sure to deliver his message before tending to his injured foot."

"I'd forgotten that," says Catherine.

As they admire the statue, Stefano explains its long history. The original Greek statue is long gone, but the Romans preserved versions of it, copying and imitating it many times. Since then, artists around the world have continued to reproduce, imitate, and otherwise depict it, both faithfully and with variations, but always recognizably. There is even a painting—a seventeenth-century still life—that shows a plaster cast of the boy, his back to a skull and pile of bones that rest next to an artist's brushes and palette. "So you see," says Stefano, "this boy has been brought back to life many times over more than two thousand years. It will be up to Catherine to bring him back one more time—for the Uffizi."

"Would you do this now?" Mark tries not to sound too eager. Now would be perfect. It would mean time away from the whole Nico problem.

Stefano laughs. "Oh no, no. Next summer. When I hope, Mark, that you and Catherine will come stay here, in beautiful Tuscany."

Catherine gets very close to the statue and crouches to look up into the boy's face. "Mark! Look."

Mark crouches down next to a smiling Catherine. "What?"

"You haven't seen him yet, so you can't appreciate it, but this boy looks exactly like I imagine Nico will in a few years."

Mark stands up and stumbles.

"Mark, are you all right?" Catherine touches his forehead, which is damp with sweat.

"I'm fine. Stood up too fast, I guess." But his heart is racing. Something is very wrong here.

After two days in the car, they've arrived back at Giulia's, or what Catherine now refers to as "our place." Mark's dull headache could be from the traffic. He was supposed to rest when Catherine drove, and he did try to nap, but always with one eye open watching the road and one foot on the fictional brake. Or maybe the headache has come from returning to Macri, the Nico problem not only unsolved but deepened. He can't even tell—is Nico really there, or are his own nerves so shot from this whole awful lie he's living that he's seeing Nico in every boy who crosses his path? Or maybe he's hallucinating. And with that thought, that admission, he understands with a sickening flash of clarity how Catherine has been feeling, how he has made Catherine feel with his deception.

Mark carries one suitcase from the car to the cottage while Catherine carries the other, walking a foot or so ahead and to his right. When she drops the key and stoops to pick it up, Mark gets a quick view of Nico standing off to the side in the middle distance. The child looks straight at Mark, his face blank, his stare blunt, stopping Mark in his tracks for a long, stomach-turning moment. But Mark recovers and continues to walk, glancing back several times at Nico, whose intent stare does not waver. Mark quickens his pace to catch up to Catherine. "Hey, Cath, everything OK?"

"Hm? Yeah. Why?"

"I saw you stop . . ." And I wondered how you missed seeing that child over there.

"Oh, yeah. I dropped the key."

Beads of sweat cover Mark's forehead. What had been an ordinary headache before has grown into a throbbing assault on his skull. "Cath?"

"Yeah?" Catherine is busy trying to reattach an ornate brass knob to the key chain.

"I—Nothing." Mark looks over his shoulder and, as he was sure would be the case, Nico is gone.

The cool part of the day is gone, and the summer heat is building by the time Mark drags himself out of bed. What he wouldn't give for an air conditioner in this bedroom. What he wouldn't give for their own bedroom back in Brooklyn.

It's no surprise that Catherine is already up and probably in her studio. The tables have turned: now he's the one with nightmares, waking up every night in the week they've been back drenched in sweat and heart racing. Luckily, Catherine had accepted his explanation, given his lack of appetite as well, that the problem must be viral or something he ate. But she's getting worried about his recent weird behavior, and so is he.

Trashed from the past several weeks of seeing Nico wherever he goes, the idea of what might be coming today exhausts him. He goes through the motions of showering and dressing, almost finishing before he's even conscious of starting, and walks out to the kitchen. Of course, there's no coffee to reheat because Catherine has taken to dumping it now that Giulia has let her know what a crime it is to drink leftover coffee. A little crime doesn't sound so bad right now. As he grinds the beans and boils water, he begins what is already the third go-round of the day of fruitless obsessing about how to deal with this mess. Something his mother used to say to them when he and his brother were kids keeps going through his mind: "You've made your bed, now lie in it."

He has the rest of this wretched day and all of tomorrow before he needs to be presentable enough to meet with potential clients as something other than a pale, sweaty guy with shaky hands who sees little boys around corners. That kid! What does he want? How does he get where he gets to? He must want to intimidate Mark and make him suffer for lying to Catherine. But what if it's more than that? It feels like more. Why else would the kid track him down in Florence, for God's sake? Or halfway up Mount-Goddamn-Etna. What ordinary—no, what normal—child would do that? Or *could*? If it's even the same boy every time—if he isn't just losing his mind.

It was bad enough before, but the day they'd come home was hard to ignore. Nico had been right there, but Catherine hadn't noticed. Unless she's gas-lighting Mark. Unless she knows he lied and is getting even. But that's not at all like Catherine. Still, every time before, he's managed to convince himself that there was a reason Catherine didn't notice Nico or whatever boy *looked* like Nico that day. But yesterday—that's tough. He's terrified and not certain of what. He's not even sure the kid is there most of the time, if he's honest with himself. The thing that rattles him most is that he is forced to at least entertain the idea that Catherine is right and Nico is a ghost.

Mark stops when he realizes he's pacing and possibly speaking out loud, that his breath is so ragged and so harsh that anyone who saw him would think he was having a heart attack. That last part's crazy. Of course the child is there. Of course he's no ghost. There *are* no ghosts. Catherine didn't see him the other day because the sun was behind him. There was a glare; that's all. Catherine's shorter than he is by a good half foot. Surely that made a difference in her view. He's wasting so much time and energy on this ridiculous crap. He's got to pull himself together and go out to see Catherine.

Throughout the entire walk to the barn, he shakes his hands and arms, trying to get rid of the jittery sensation, grown all too familiar, that radiates from his heart to his fingertips. His stomach is in an uproar. He can't recall—did he eat breakfast? At the barn, he stops before going through the doors, looking in to find Catherine working, and from all appearances, content and happy. Nico, who sits on the floor playing, looks up at Mark straightaway. There's that face, that stare. That artless, frank, accusing, obnoxious stare. Words play through his mind in a childish chant—"malevolent, malodorous, malfeasant, malignant." The image of an imposing evil witch—from a movie he watched as a child, one he can't name and hasn't thought of in thirty years—appears in his mind's eye. It is only a moment before the witch looms over him, laughing, and his brain fills with a distorted sound, like music from a sad carousel slowed to a draggy dirge. Now, words from a nursery rhyme repeat in his head, slurred and deformed, ugly and threatening: "Ladybug, ladybug, fly away home. Your house is on fire. Your children will burn." He clutches his head to make it stop, and when it does, he takes a moment to calm himself, covering his eyes to think. Nico has seen him, but Catherine has not. He checks, and she still shows no awareness of his presence, so he backs away, each footstep silent, ready to raise his hand and wave if Catherine should look up, relieved beyond words when she doesn't. He can't deal with this right now. When he's sure he's out of view of the barn, he turns back toward the cottage, defeated, hiding from his wife, doubting his own sanity but certain of one thing—he's brought all this, whatever it is, on himself.

With the sun high overhead, a soaking-wet and exhausted Mark wades onto the northern shore of Mozia, Catherine a few steps ahead. Last night had been better than the previous half dozen—only one nightmare, and he'd gotten back to sleep after a single glass of wine. Catherine hadn't ever noticed he was up. Mark drops to the sand beside her. "Well, it can be done."

"I didn't think quite so much of the last part of the road would be a full three feet under. It's *hard* walking in water that deep."

"We're taking the ferry back."

"You won't get an argument from me. But just so you know, it isn't some big ferry. It's a dinky little thing."

Mark has just nodded off, but he jerks awake when Catherine stands up and takes a futile stab at brushing the coarse sand from the back of her wet jeans. "This isn't coming off anytime soon. We're going to look like mummies with all the dirt and dust here."

Dragging himself to standing, Mark gives his pants a few lackadaisical brushes. Who's going to see them, anyway? Catherine said the island is nearly empty. "You say where we're headed isn't far from here?"

"A really short walk. Come on."

Where does she get the stamina in this heat and humidity? Only the coolness of his sodden clothes keeps him going. The path, though, is beautiful enough to make him forget his discomfort. He suspects they are going to the cemetery she mentioned the other night. "Cath, look at these ruins over here." It looks like there are some good places to sit, and he's pretty sure it's not the damn cemetery.

"Can we do it on the way back? I really want to be sure you see this and have enough time to appreciate it." It's not too long before Catherine stops at a flat, open area. "Here it is. A Phoenician cemetery. Isn't that crazy? Why isn't it fenced off? Covered with swarms of archaeologists? Nothing is protected. From anything."

Mark squats to look at the pottery on the ground. "These jugs—urns—you say they're for ashes?"

"Let's go sit over here, and I'll tell you everything I know."

When she's done, Mark is as shaken as a sinner at a tent meeting. "I'm stunned. I vaguely remember something about Phoenicians and child sacrifice—and, of course, you mentioned it the other day—but this is way too real. These people did this to their own kids." He looks out over the field of sad, small jars, jammed at odd angles all around the site. Their wide, round openings look like so many mouths set in *O*s of bewildered surprise, or like hollow eyes forlorn with the heart-break of the innocent. The thought that each one represents a dead child, betrayed and abandoned by the two people that child trusted most—it overwhelms him. No wonder this had moved Catherine so. It's understandable she might overreact. Anyone might. Mark turns his head at the soft sound of scrabbling in the dirt. An electric green lizard, out of place among this field of somber browns and tans, runs into a half-buried urn.

"Mark, don't you see? This has to be where Nico is from. This empty, desperate place—this is what he calls home."

"As sad as this is, Cath, I don't see that at all."

"I never told you this, but a couple of weeks ago, I was doing a drawing—of that stele over there. Nico corrected it. He knew that stele so well, he was able to fix the details."

"That doesn't prove anything. Maybe he comes here with his friends."

"You're talking about him as if he were an ordinary child, not one you looked right through. Twice, Mark. Twice!"

"There has to be an explanation for that."

"OK. Let's say there is. How does he get between here and Macri, then? We showed today—he can't walk, not at his height. And anyway, he's not wet when he arrives, so he doesn't swim either."

"I have no idea, Catherine, I—this is confusing. Don't take this the wrong way, but I think we're going to look back on it and laugh someday. Because Nico as a sacrificed child simply makes no sense. The situation here—it's tragic. It's sickening. And I understand—it makes you want to do something about it. But we can't. And it has nothing to do with Nico. To think that it does—it's crazy. I don't know what else to call it. Even if I thought he was a ghost, which I don't."

Catherine's tone becomes all business. "I want to stay in Sicily, Mark. I've given it a lot of thought, and I don't want to go back to New

York. Not yet. Maybe after a while, we could go back and take Nico with us, but not now."

"Take Nico with us? What are you talking about?"

"I want us to make a life here with Nico. His parents threw him away like trash, cheated him out of his life. We can make that right. We can stay here and give a needy little boy a chance he never had. We can raise him like our own son."

Mark stands up and looks down at Catherine. "Do you hear yourself?" He paces, rubbing his face. "Stay here? Adopt a ghost boy? And live where? On a goat farm or something?" He stops and looks back at Catherine. "Tell me, if Nico is a ghost, well, how does that work exactly? What if I *never* see him? Do you expect me to be happy spending my life living in the middle of nowhere with an invisible son?"

"I think we can make it work, Mark. I—we—got chosen by Nico for a reason."

"Yeah. To do penance for the sins of the Phoenicians. That's nuts! The blood of those children is not on our hands."

Catherine stands and touches Mark's arm. He turns to face her. Her voice softens. "He's a child. We have to at least try."

"Look, what we have to do is go back to New York. We have a life there. And I haven't wanted to tell you until I was more sure it's going to be doable, but I've been working on a plan—through the firm at home—to bring American investment here. Not just limit our involvement to providing plans and working with builders, but bring money to the table too. The firm would get healthy fees for setting up the investment. And with more capital available to the farm owners, they can afford to do more. We can modernize some of these places and set them up for tourism in ways some of these folks can only dream of. Not just Roberto, but others too, a lot of others."

Catherine is shaking her head.

"Listen to me, Cath. We can make a lot of money on this. Us personally. Our life could be something—something you can't even picture. I've met people—you'd love them. They'd love you. And they have it all, Cath. Time home in New York. Time here in Italy. We could live where we want in New York and come back to Italy all the time. Whenever we wanted."

"And visit your new Club Meds?"

"That's not fair. That's not at all what I have in mind. Look, these are people who want to keep their family land, but they're struggling. They need income from the land to make it work. They can't have only one or two guests and make a go of it. They need to be able to accommodate more people—"

"So you'll build a—a—fifty-room Holiday Inn where their barn used to be."

"No!" Mark's frustration grows as he sees that Catherine isn't even listening. "Some places need to put up four guests. Some want room for as many as a dozen. Maybe a place to serve breakfast. Or even dinner using the produce of their own farms. But in every case, the new buildings will be modest. They'll match the rural nature of the originals."

"I never thought you would be willing to destroy authentic character for profit—"

"You're passing judgment, and you haven't even seen what I'm proposing. If you'd just listen for a minute—"

"It wouldn't matter. I like these places the way they are, and I don't want to make money by ruining them. Why would you? I don't even know who you are anymore."

All Mark can read on Catherine's face is disdain. Never in his life has he felt so boxed in. He's furious—with Catherine, with himself, and with that damn kid. He drops his head and rubs his eyes to soothe the pain behind them. When he looks up, he sees what he's been fearing he would see all day. Near the road and to his right, Nico stands. Terror blends in with the anger, and a fuzzy buzzing begins in his ears along with fractured, distorted bits of the nursery rhyme that has been haunting him since yesterday—"Your house is on fire . . . your house is on fire . . ." His entire body gears up to run, a horrible sensation he does his best to hide. It's close to more than he can take. When the boy meets his gaze, the pounding in his head grows more ferocious than he thought possible, and he's quite sure he's about to faint for the first time in his life. He turns back toward Catherine, who shows no sign of noticing Nico. She looks so sad and so hurt that he loathes himself again, an all-too-familiar feeling lately. With a few moments of clarity to figure things out, he could get a handle on this whole fucking fiasco. If he doesn't come apart first. If he doesn't have a stroke on this godforsaken island.

Things have gone too far. There are only two ways out of this wreckage. He can undermine Catherine's self-confidence and make her believe she's imagined Nico—that's one way. But he'd have to be a heartless monster to do that. The only other way is to admit he can see the boy.

They need to get in step again, and he needs Catherine back, the way it used to be. Catherine is the one he wants to go to, to tell her about Nico's unnerving presence in his life, real or imagined. To seek her comfort. More than that, he needs Catherine to need him again. He can fix it if she'll forgive him—something he's never worried about before. Then he can meet Nico, and surely the boy will leave him alone after that. And even if it's only a guilty conscience that's been stalking him, well, coming clean about seeing Nico would take care of that too.

Catherine comes in and goes straight to the sink to wash the clay from her hands. Even after ten years together, small things about her move him—the slight asymmetry of her mouth, her unconscious habit of rubbing her right elbow when she's thinking, the way she stands with one hip to the side as she does right now.

"Hey, come be with me, Cath. Please?"

Looking tentative, Catherine sits on the opposite end of the couch, turning to lean her back against the lumpy arm, feet up on the cushions, forming a barrier between them. Mark takes her feet into his lap and massages them. "Tired?"

"That feels good. Thanks."

"Any time."

"How have we gotten to this point, Mark? Like strangers."

"It's my fault. All of it."

"No, I—"

"No, wait. Listen." Mark stops massaging and hooks his fingers behind his neck, bringing his elbows together. "I'm not good at this sort of thing, and this is really hard, so please just listen, all right?"

"You're scaring me." Catherine withdraws her legs from Mark's lap and sits up straighter.

"Cath, you know you mean the world to me, and I would never do anything on purpose to hurt you. But I have. Not because I wanted to hurt you, but because I was stupid. Stupid and childish."

"What is this about?"

"I have seen Nico."

Her eyes awaken with what he recognizes as a mixture of joy and relief. "I knew you would. When?"

"That day weeks ago, in the studio. When I looked right at him? Well, I did see him. And the next time too."

"Are you—are you saying you lied to me?"

"It wasn't so much a lie. Or maybe, I guess, it was. But I did it without thinking. As a joke."

"A joke?" Catherine speaks as if the word is unfamiliar, perhaps not English.

"It seemed kind of funny. You know, all those times I'd missed him before. By a hair sometimes. When I did see him, almost before I knew I was doing it, I said I didn't. I guess you'd say on a whim."

Catherine stands. She wraps her arms around herself as if to ward off sudden cold, shakes her head no, and appears to be speaking to herself. "A joke. On a whim."

"I let it go too far. Way too far. But I didn't know how to stop."

"And you tried to make me think I was having some kind of breakdown as a joke too? What is wrong with you?" She goes to the window.

Mark joins Catherine, hands in his pockets. He avoids looking out, fearing Nico will be there. "I can't even explain it to myself. I behaved like an idiot. I mean, I wanted to fix it, and I kept making it worse. It was embarrassingly juvenile. And I am truly, truly sorry." He puts his hand on her arm, but she jerks away.

"I don't believe it." Her voice is angry, bitter.

"I don't blame you, but honestly, I'm sorrier than I've ever been in my life."

"No, no. I mean I don't believe that you saw Nico. You must think I'm an idiot. It makes no sense."

"Catherine, please—"

"You know what I think? I think you finally comprehend—I finally got it through to you—that I want to stay here and take care of Nico. You're trying to make me feel there's nothing special about him. Or my relationship to him. To make me feel foolish. So I'll pack up and go back to New York with you and forget the whole thing. Well, it won't work."

Mark pulls out a kitchen chair and sits on it backward, facing Catherine, who has gone to the sink for a glass of water. "I am telling you the truth. I saw Nico in your studio both those times." He's amazed by how calm he sounds, because he feels the anger threatening to bubble up and spill out into the room like a river.

"I don't accept that. Why should I? Either you were lying then or you're lying now, and there was no reason for you to lie then. Understand this, Mark. I am amazingly lucky that Nico has come back to our time, to *me*. And I intend to adopt him."

Mark gets up with such force that the chair tumbles sideways. "What are you doing, Catherine? Have you stopped to look at what you're doing to us with these bizarre ideas? Nico is an ordinary child. Some local kid with a family of his own. You have to stop thinking of him as a ghost or a child we can adopt. Or both—that's the craziest thought of all—that he's a ghost, and we have some kind of 'calling' to adopt him and right the wrongs of the bloody Phoenicians. I've never heard anything so absurd."

"Your mind is closed, Mark. I can't talk to you if all I get back is preconceived notions."

Mark had come into this conversation knowing he had no real right to be angry, and determined to control his temper. He's the one in the wrong. He's the one who moments ago hit her with this shameful confession. Willing himself to hold it together, recognizing this as a crucial moment, he faces Catherine, hands on top of his head like a suspect about to be frisked. "Catherine, love, I'm sorrier than I know how to say. I did an awful thing to you. All the talk in the world won't change that."

"This is a nightmare."

"Look." He places a hand softly on each side of Catherine's arms and is grateful when she does not pull away, although she remains rigid, her face unyielding. "Let me repeat what you said to me a few weeks ago. Don't say anything right now. Think it over. Think it over and remember—I'm still Mark, just Mark who made a really stupid mistake."

She wants to believe this ghost story, that's all. She'll see the reality after she's had some time to think alone. Surely she'll come to her senses then.

TWENTY-NINE

CATHERINE

As Catherine walks out to Giulia's car, she rummages through her purse for her wallet. This time, she'd like to be sure she has it *before* she gets to the market. Although no one had seemed upset last time. She'd left that day, groceries in hand, and waved off with a reassurance that she should pay next time. She could get used to living this way. She locates the wallet and closes her purse, surprised when she looks up to see Mark's car parked in its usual spot. She thought Mark had left to do research of some kind in the Marsala library.

Looking back toward the main house, Catherine spots Mark and Giulia in the distance. They stand close together, engaged in conversation, and she winces at the thought that perhaps Giulia knows they are having problems. Could she have overheard sharp words between them? Does she want reassurance that everything is still all right—that they aren't planning to up and leave in the middle of the night? Or maybe she's concerned that they're the kind of people who throw things or damage furniture when they get angry. But it seems more likely that Giulia would have brought such questions up with Catherine.

Unless—maybe Mark is warning Giulia that Catherine needs special handling, that she thinks she's friends with a ghost. After all, he went behind her back before, telling Giulia she "wasn't feeling well" and needed looking in on. Who knows what he'd said then? But no. All of it is silly. There hasn't been anything loud or nasty here for Giulia to overhear, and Mark has no reason to want Giulia thinking Catherine is a little off. That would embarrass him. A flaky wife does not fit in well with Mark's self-image. Probably, he had a question for Giulia about using the library, that's all.

They seem to be finishing up, so Catherine slips into the car and drives off, hoping she's escaped unseen. When she reaches the little market, she pulls sharply into the last open space on the street, jamming two wheels up onto the narrow walk. She steps out of the car and sizes up its perch—somewhat impertinent and worthy of a local. She's still congratulating herself on a job well done when she hears someone calling her name.

Catherine turns to see Sandra sitting alone at the café a few doors down from the market. Sandra is waving Catherine over, so she pockets her shopping list and joins her at the tiny, round table.

"Have time for a coffee?" Sandra pulls her espresso cup closer to make room. "I feel like I haven't seen you in a long time."

Funny, but to Catherine it feels as if she sees Sandra most of the times she's in town, although she enjoys her company. "I can't stay too long, but sure." Catherine signals to the waiter, who nods once and sets off for the espresso machine.

"I have the day free. Kenneth has the kids, and I'm here to do a little thinking."

Catherine laughs. "You mean this street is quieter than your house?"

"Not exactly. But none of the noise here has my name on it, if you know what I mean." Sandra looks down and fiddles with her cup. "I am jealous of you and that studio of yours, though. So peaceful and quiet." She looks up at Catherine with her unnerving smile. "No one out there but you." Is it Catherine's imagination, or is Sandra gauging her reaction?

"It is a great space." Catherine watches Sandra's face for any change of expression, but none is obvious. "I feel lucky we found it."

"I feel lucky I found *you*. I think we're kindred spirits, you know? If only you were staying—moving here. I think we could work together. And—oh, I don't know, I play this little game in my head where you and Mark have a couple of kids, and we take care of them for you and you watch ours, and we're all great friends."

Deciding to avoid most of what Sandra has brought up, Catherine says, "Work together? How so?" She stirs sugar into her espresso as if this is an activity that precludes any eye contact.

"Well, I had an idea for a series of children's books, and I've been discussing it with a college friend who works for an educational publisher. He's really excited about it. And they have a relationship with some major museums, so that would help, you know?"

"I'm afraid you've lost me. Museums?"

"The idea is to take maybe eight famous paintings and do a book on each. But instead of the usual photographs of the work—although we'd have photos too—I want to show the works come to life. With drawings. Drawings I can't make—and that's where you could come in. In my fantasy, anyway. I want kids to see paintings and maybe even statues as real—through beautiful drawings. You know, Mona Lisa walking down the street. In her kitchen. Brushing her hair before bed. Figures from Vermeer, Holbein, Van Gogh, Degas—I want to tell stories about those wonderful people they created. I think it would encourage kids to look at art in a new way."

"That is an amazing idea. I'm not sure I'm the one—"

"The project is only in its infancy now. And who knows—it might never happen. But, when I think about it, I can't help thinking how great it would be to work with you."

"You know, you could do a lot with classical statues too. Mythological figures." Catherine laughs. "A Day in the Life of Mercury." She sighs. "I hope you get this off the ground. I know a couple of people

I could put you in touch with. For the illustrations. It makes me a little jealous because it sounds like fun, but I don't think Mark and I will be here all that much longer."

"Oh, don't say that! It makes me too sad." Sandra smiles and squeezes Catherine's hand. "Let's not think about it. I mean, things change. A year ago, would you have ever pictured yourself right here, right now, having this conversation?"

Catherine tenses, again wondering—could Sandra mean more than she's saying? "For sure, no."

"See? Really. You just never know what life has in store, do you?"

THIRTY

MARK

Showered, shaved, and in his best suit, Mark still feels like death warmed over as he approaches Paola's desk in the Palermo office. If he can just get through the morning, just buy a little time, he can pull himself together.

"I hate to bother you with this," he says, looking as warm and friendly as he can muster, "but would you mind canceling all my appointments starting tomorrow and through next week? I've been down with a really nasty flu or something, and I need some time to recuperate."

"Of course." Paola narrows her eyes. She scrutinizes his face until what seems like a burst of embarrassment causes her to look away. What has made her so uncomfortable—her own open staring or the fear and disarray she sees in him?

"If you have my mail, I'll take it into the conference room, and when I'm done with any replies, I'll head out of here and let the good Sicilian sunshine work its magic." He smiles, an ordinary guy who's under the weather.

He sits and sorts through his mail, looking for the envelope from Seth. He opens it, scans the letter—pretty much the same old thing, every couple of weeks like clockwork—folds it, and places it in his pocket. After he reads the rest of his mail and jots a few notes of reply, he brings all but Seth's letter out to Paola. "If you wouldn't mind taking care of these—file the letters and mail the replies?"

"Right away," she says. She hesitates. "Signor Lindquist? If I might?"

"Yes?"

"You look like you still do not feel very good. What we do in my *villaggio*—we take an egg—not cooked—and put it on the floor next to the bed. For one week. It will take in all the badness and sickness in the room. Then after one week, you take the egg outside, far from the house, and you dig a hole. Hatch the egg—this is the right word—hatch?"

"I think you mean crack? Crack open?"

"Yes, yes. Crack it. It will smell very terrible from all the bad things it has taken away from the room. You bury this egg in the hole." She shrugs, as if nothing could be simpler "This should cure the illness."

"Oh. Well, thank you." Mark can't think of a thing to say about this.

"You are welcome. It will make you better, unless—" She leans in, lowering her voice. "Unless someone has put on you the *malocchio*—the evil eye. You can tell if you have received this curse in a very easy way. Fill a small bowl with water and drop into it three drops—three exactly—of olive oil. If the oil comes together to make a shape of an eye, then you know you have this problem, and someone in the *villaggio* can help you with the way to fight it. But meantime, please take this as a little gift." She opens her drawer and takes out a small box. She lifts the cover to show Mark a *corna* on a chain, before handing the box to Mark. "This will make sure you do not get a new evil eye put on you."

"Oh. I've read about these. Thanks. Thanks again." He fears he might have overdone his attempt to appear gracious. It's possible that he came across as having a sincere interest in this stuff, and that could come back to bite him. Who knows what Paola will come up with next time he's here?

As Mark gets into his car, he tosses the box into the backseat. He takes Seth's letter from his pocket, unlocks the glove box, and puts the letter into a manila envelope along with all the others. Saving them might be pointless, although it's possible he'll need to show them to Catherine for some reason in the future. Probably not, but at least they're safe here, and he can always get rid of them later.

Mark leans back in the seat, aware of the box in the back. He turns and retrieves it, opening it for a more careful look. The delicacy of the extended fingers, complete with minuscule nails, and the detail of the rest of the hand are impressive, as if it had been important to get this right. He laughs to himself—maybe the evil eye won't stay away if the hand isn't convincing enough. The chain is long and heavy. This must be designed for a man to wear, hidden down under his shirt. Does Paola have a drawer full of different versions? Suitable for every man, woman, and child she might find to be in need of protection?

Mark coils the necklace back into its cotton bed and replaces the box top. He'll never wear it, but he can't throw it away either. Unlocking the glove compartment, he places the box next to the envelope of Seth's letters. Reluctant to start back, knowing he has to face Catherine and the impossible situation he's created, Mark once again leans back in his seat. He watches a caterpillar lower itself on a thin filament of silk from a tree branch overhead onto the windshield of the car. Feet on the glass, it meanders first in one direction, then another. "I feel your pain, buddy. On the outside, looking in—that's how this island makes me feel. But maybe we're both better off that way." He shakes his head. A receptionist who's a part-time witch, eggs on the floor, oil on water, and a magical necklace. He just can't get out of Sicily fast enough.

◆ ◆ ◆

Mark arranges some flowers in a jar and tidies up the kitchen before he goes into the bedroom to change. An unfortunate by-product of his preparing the menu Giulia suggested—Pesto Trapanese, broccoli di rabe, and blood-orange salad—is a psychedelic array of green and orange splotches on his shirt. That won't do. This evening has to be perfect. The quiet around here for the last two days has not been good. If they don't connect, Catherine might continue to withdraw. A surprise dinner with wine and candlelight—it's a cliché, but it can't hurt.

Back in the kitchen, Mark listens for Catherine's car. He's not sure why she went into town today, but she said she'd be back by seven, and she's always been punctual, at least before she decided to "go Italian." Shortly after seven, he hears the sound of tires and the slam of a car door. The evening is still bright and beautiful, ideal for dinner alfresco. When she comes in the door, he smiles at her look of surprise.

"Hello. I am Mark, and I will be your chef, waiter, busboy, and dinner companion for this evening." He bows from the waist. "Smell good in here?"

She puts her packages on the kitchen counter. "Smells wonderful." She sounds cautious. "You've gone to a lot of trouble."

"I hope you don't mind eating a little early. I thought it would be fun to dine outside—notice it's 'dining' when *I* cook—while the sun is up." He hopes his attempt at being light is the right approach. "And we can linger. And talk. It's all set up on the side patio."

"Let me go get cleaned up a bit, and I'll come out."

Catherine disappears into the bedroom, and Mark brings the food and flowers outdoors. He's pouring wine into her glass when she joins him.

"Looks professional." Catherine takes a seat.

"I have many talents you don't know about."

Mark serves them both. Catherine is acting more engaged but not saying much. To break the silence, he says, "I was talking to Giulia. Her nephew was here for the day."

"I think I saw him as I was driving out."

"Yeah. He has some kind of windsurfing *thing* he does. I asked Giulia what it was, and she said, 'Eh, he enjoys this, like all the lovers of the wind.' Funny turn of phrase."

"It is. It's a little bit off somehow, yet you know what she means."

They eat in silence except for a few compliments, seemingly genuine, from Catherine. When they're through, Mark says, "Let's leave this and take our wine and the candles—I put matches in my pocket here somewhere—and go sit over there and watch the sunset."

Catherine moves the pair of lounge chairs to face west. "What an evening. Look at that color on the water." Smudges of burgundy shimmer on the surface of the sea like blood spilled from the ruddy face of the sun.

Mark sits in the chair next to her and sighs, stretching his legs out, crossing his ankles and folding his hands behind his head. As the low, wispy clouds grow more bloodshot, everything takes on an eerie coppery flush. "Cath?"

"Mmm?"

"We can't keep going like this. Not talking. It's been like living with a shadow the last few days. Won't you tell me what you're thinking?"

Catherine sips her wine and holds the nearly empty glass toward the sun. Rotating the stem between her fingers, she opens and closes one eye, then the other. Tiny red pixies of light play on her cheeks and nose. Abruptly, they look to Mark like spatters of blood. He squeezes his eyes shut. When he reopens them, the gory droplets are sparkles again.

"Are you never going to talk to me again?"

She puts the glass down. "No. It's not that. I'm not trying to freeze you out or anything. I just . . ." She turns her head away and appears lost in thought.

"Don't stop there."

"It's just that I can't stop thinking about why. I mean, I accept that you've seen Nico now. I don't think that changes the fact that he's a ghost. But I don't get why you would do what you say you did as a joke. It makes no sense. You're not cruel, and that would be such a cruel thing to do, I—"

"I tried to explain—"

"I don't see you making sadistic jokes. But I don't really see you claiming that you did if you didn't. That's every bit as heartless. So, I have to accept that one way or the other, you've lied, and one way or the other, you've been cruel."

The sun is almost set now, and Mark lights the pair of candles he has placed on the low table between them, the slight tremor in his hand a remnant of his shock at the sight of Catherine's blood-flecked face. No longer painted by the dramatic sunset, Catherine's skin now appears monochrome in the dim flicker of candlelight. Mark lowers his hands to his sides and grips the chair's armrests. "You're right. I wouldn't play a stupid, hurtful joke like that. And I didn't." He can't read anything on her face. Has she understood him? "I did see Nico—both those times. I didn't deny it as a joke, but because—I said it because you were growing so attached to him. And I was straight-up afraid of losing you. Jealous, maybe? I don't know. That sounds petty. And maybe it was."

He waits, her silence unnerving him more and more by the minute. "I didn't plan it. The thought of—well, of lying like that—it never crossed my mind. I just did it. Like a knee-jerk reaction to a sudden danger I felt—to you and to me. I didn't want to lose us, Catherine. I did it because I cared so much about you. Care—I still care."

Catherine draws her knees up under her chin and wraps her arms around her legs. "You always come to a new place and expect to find things. But not something like this."

"I don't understand."

"What you said—it's like finding a different Mark."

She sounds sad, not angry as he'd been expecting. And he feels checked, uncertain of how to make matters better, not worse. He waits, but Catherine doesn't look at him, much less speak. "Is that all you can say?"

"I think you know I care about you too. About us. I've loved you since about fifteen minutes after we first met. I can't even tell you how much I want to believe that you did what you did out of caring for me. For us."

"Believe it, then."

"God, Mark. Don't try to make it sound simple. As if this is something *I'm* doing. Something *I* can choose to fix or wish away. When you 'came clean' the other day, now I know it was only partway. You kept some of the story to yourself. And that's the good interpretation. Better than the other—that you make it up as you need it."

"Catherine, please, I swear. You have to believe me. I've put it all out there now."

"How can I believe that? How will I not always wonder what else you're either hiding or ready to invent to suit your purposes? Honestly, I'm lost. Some days, I make myself try to ignore it. I pretend that there hasn't been this gigantic earthquake in our lives. I—I act happy to be happy, you know? Because I want it to go away. But other days . . ." She lowers her voice to a whisper. "I feel like a widow. The loss—it's—it's devastating. I know then that I can't really wish it away."

"I got us into this. What can I do to get us out? Please—tell me."

"So you can make up a story you think I want to hear?" She sighs. "I wonder, did I ever really know you? I can't even tell anymore."

Mark opens his eyes to feel Catherine stroking his cheek, exploring his face. Even in the total darkness, his first instinct is to smile, but then his stomach drops, and his smile ebbs away. Something is off. How can her hand be reaching from the right when she's sleeping to his left?

"Cath?" He thinks he's spoken, but he can't be sure. Lying perfectly still on his back, he tries again. "Catherine?" This time, the memory lingers in his throat. He lifts his left arm and makes a slow, cautious pass through the space between them. He touches nothing, finds no arm reaching over his body.

Cold sweat erupts on his neck, chest, and face. The exploring hands are on his mouth now, touching his lips, covering his nose a whisper too long to be comfortable. These are small hands. They bring a whiff of the outdoors, of the sea and the earth—the salty, unwashed scent of childhood. Nico? He'd locked the door himself before bed. Nico couldn't have gotten in. It must be a dream, that's all. He'll wake up soon enough. But he doesn't, and the hands continue their fierce intrusion.

His attempt to sit up is met with a rush of movement, and now there's a weight on his chest. Oh God, what if this is a heart attack? Or a stroke? It's as if all the air has bled from the room. Gasping, suffocating, he struggles, and a warm dampness appears on his cheeks. He must be crying. But now, a familiar wet-coin odor reaches his nostrils. Blood. It's blood. He squelches an overpowering urge to vomit as the hands slowly, slowly, slowly paint his face with the warm, sticky liquid. Again he tries calling out to Catherine but can't. He howls, but no sound comes. The blood is in his mouth now, and in his eyes and nose. His internal frenzy and outward thrashing grow as leaden terror settles itself in his heart. He feels gagged, bound, blindfolded, and is about to admit defeat—to whom? for what?—when, without warning, the hands stop and the weight lifts from his chest. Bursting from the bed, he fights his way against nothing to the bathroom, where he scrabbles for the light switch and runs to the mirror. His eyes are grotesque with terror and panic, and sweat coats his face and neck, forming runnels on his cheeks and forehead. The moisture soaks his T-shirt. But there is no blood. Was it a nightmare? A hallucination? Still breathing like a drowning man, he looks out into the bedroom. In the shaft of light from the bathroom, he can see that, at least now, no one is there, no one but Catherine, who is still sound asleep. He closes the door without a sound, slips to the bathroom floor, laces his fingers in his hair, and weeps.

◆　◆　◆

Sitting across the breakfast table from Catherine, Mark wonders how he must look to her these days. He doesn't even recognize himself in the mirror anymore, especially after the horrible event of a few nights ago. "Event"—that's all he can bring himself to call it. Not that he ever plans to talk about it.

Catherine puts aside the letter she's been reading. "Stefano says everything is moving along. It's looking set for next summer."

"Good." He almost said it will be nice for her to be back here, but then Catherine would launch into her speech about how she's not leaving. They haven't talked about it much. They haven't talked about anything much. She's suspicious of whatever Mark says anyway, and her main focus has been—of course—Nico. The boy hasn't been back to see Catherine all week, which is fine with Mark but appears to be killing Catherine.

"Mark?"

"Hmm?"

"When was the last time you shaved? Are you out of blades or something?"

Mark rubs his chin and cheeks, and the stiff bristles scratch his fingers. "Out? No. I still have a lot of what I brought." In fact, the box is still at least half-full. With a shudder, he fights off the momentary image of running his finger across the steely edges of a phalanx of blades, his flesh shredding to threads, blood pooling in the bottom of the box. This isn't the first impromptu gruesome thought that has come into his head recently, another reason to get out of this place, the sooner the better.

"Are you growing a beard, then?"

For some reason, these questions are getting to him, and there's no reason they should be. "I'm taking a break. Taking advantage of a week at home. What's the big deal?" The short answer, really, is "Who gives a shit?" but maybe Catherine does. She *is* showing some interest in him now. That's refreshing.

"Mark, you're sure there isn't something else—some other reason?"

"What's with all the questions? Are there a lot more? Because maybe I should get an attorney before we go on."

"I just wanted to be sure there isn't . . . You seem not yourself. Depressed, maybe."

"I simply haven't felt like bothering. OK?"

"Well, would you mind shaving, then? For me? Because, I'm afraid when Nico comes back, he might not recognize you and get scared before I can explain."

Mark laughs—too loudly, he can tell. Catherine looks like a puritan in a porn shop, a thought that only makes him laugh more.

"Mark, stop!"

He slams both palms on the table, causing Catherine to jump. "OK. No more laughing." The crazy man promising not to laugh at the crazy woman. If their life doesn't qualify as a shambles, what does?

"I'm glad you find it all so amusing."

Mark leans back in his chair. "Well, maybe it was that I mistook your concern for Nico as concern for me."

"I *am* concerned about you, but I don't know what to say anymore."

"But you're more concerned about Nico."

"Not more. I'm worried about him. That's all. It's been—"

"I know, I know, I know. Nearly a week."

"What if something happened to him?"

"Now *that's* funny. What can happen to a ghost? Didn't it all pretty much happen already?"

Catherine looks away.

"Do you realize all you talk about is Nico? A kid who had nothing better to do for a while, and now he's gone back to his friends. Let it go, Catherine."

"He's important to me."

"Important. He's important. Cooking is important. Baking, knitting, dressing like some Sicilian peasant from the eighteen hundreds— all important. Me? That's a laugh. I don't have any idea what the hell is wrong with you. I don't know what happened to the sophisticated woman I married. You know, the one I could take with me to meet important people around Italy without being embarrassed. The one who would fit in, not stand out like a sore thumb and talk about nothing but her latest backward obsession."

"I know you're angry, Mark. And depressed. I see that. I'm not even going to engage with you about what you just said. Maybe later when—"

"But you'd talk about little fucking Nico any old time, right?"

"We can help him."

Mark stands up, walks to the couch, and drops down, lying flat on his back, holding both sides of his throbbing head. "We? Where are you getting this 'we' from? This is one hundred percent about you. I want nothing to do with it."

"I know you won't feel that way as soon as you get to know him."

Mark walks back to the table in a few long strides. He leans down, palms on the surface, and looks straight into Catherine's eyes. "I will never change my mind. And here's why." He makes no attempt to control the ugliness of his anger. "You haven't seen Nico all week? Well, you know what? I have. Several times. Mostly outside, but once he was in the barn, and you didn't even know. Once—" He straightens up and paces. "Once he was in our bedroom."

Catherine gasps and covers her mouth with both hands.

"And what's worse? I've seen him all over the fucking place ever since that first day in the barn, when I said he wasn't there." Even he can hear his tone playing around the edges of raving. "He must not have liked it, because he has followed me every-damn-where I've gone. Riposto, Etna, Segesta, Marsala—oh, and Erice. He was all over Erice."

Catherine hasn't moved. "He stands there and looks at me with that stare. It's threatening, Catherine. I don't know who or what he is, but I am so damn strung out about it, I can't even sleep anymore." He pushes his hair back from his forehead, blotting sweat with his sleeve. "He's stalking me. Your sweet little waif is stalking me."

Jumping up from the table, Catherine stares at Mark, taking several steps backward. The look on her face is one of recognition—recognition and repulsion. Buy why? She turns and walks out of the house. Mark drops into a chair at the table and holds his head in his hands, shaking like a man on a five-day drunk.

THIRTY-ONE

SETH

March 1, 1993

Dear Notebook,
You've been great. I've been kind of dramatic sometimes, but you never laughed. Thanks. But I'm
through. There's nothing left that I want or care about.
Including myself.

I'm really pretty calm about it so I know it's the
right decision. I never did go back to Dr W but that
wouldn't have helped. I called after hours today and
left a message. Press 2 to leave a non-urgent message—
that struck me funny. Just made for someone like me.
He won't hear the message until tomorrow and it will
be too late but I wanted him to know none of this is
his fault. Nothing can fix a loser. Maybe if anybody
cares they'll give you to him, Notebook, and he'll read
this and see how badly I screwed everything up.

Speaking of being a loser, this is almost funny. I
decided to do it today because it would be exactly one
year since the fire. February 29, 1992. But you know

what I didn't think of? There *is* no February 29 this year. Only in leap years. So I even managed to fuck that up. Well what difference does it really make anyway? Just a little less drama.

I sent Catherine a letter so she knows it wasn't her fault either. I sent it to her house because hell I don't know they probably monitor her campus mail and it wouldn't even get there to her. I said that backwards. Get to her there. Yeah, I've had a lot of scotch. Pretty good scotch and in a few minutes those pills I have left from Dr W are going to be put to good use.

What a meaningless little turd of a life I lived. And I really fixed it up at the end. I can't even tell anymore what the fuck happened. Maybe Catherine's husband—Mark the Arkitekt ha ha—maybe he's right. Maybe I did stalk him and don't remember. Just how screwed up is that? But even if he made all that part up I still blew it big time with Catherine and school. And let's not forget my family. Better to shuffle off now before I meet someone else to take down. Or find another way to make a total ass of myself.

So, Notebook, this is it. It's been real.

Seth

Total since I started keeping track

Plane crashes: 1067

Natural disasters: 5078

Other disasters: 1638 (7 they say from some bomb in the World Trade Center)

Fucked Up Life: 1

THIRTY-TWO

CATHERINE

Kayaking here has dissipated some of the adrenaline surge from the morning's revelations. "He's stalking me." Mark's very words. Familiar words. Does he know that? She's not sure he knows where the truth begins and ends anymore. She *is* sure he's doing his best to make her feel she has no choice but to leave Nico and this incredible place behind for the sake of Mark's safety. He's resorted to guilt, sure that it would work because—as she now understands for the first time—it had worked before.

When Seth had continued to send letters and gifts, Catherine told Mark she planned to talk to Seth face-to-face. In his last letter, he'd said he was in therapy, and she worried that he felt wronged, given that she'd cut him off so abruptly. Maybe he needed to work something out with her to help him move on and progress toward getting well. But Mark had been opposed. Seth could be dangerous, he'd said, and Catherine should keep her priorities straight, not taking risks for someone she knew almost nothing about. Mark had seemed put out when she wasn't convinced, so she'd promised to think it over before doing anything, but she'd never gotten the chance.

She sees now that Mark's very next step had been to come to her and say that Seth had begun bothering him—harassing him, he called it. If Mark viewed her interactions with a child as a threat to their relationship, imagine how he must have felt about Seth, a young man with intelligent eyes, a boyishly appealing face, and a host of interests shared with Catherine.

At first, Mark said Seth had shown up in a handful of places, looking at Mark and walking away. Later, Mark reported that Seth's presence was growing more overt, more disconcerting, and ultimately, for reasons Mark could not fully articulate, more threatening. When Mark had used the word *stalking*, Catherine had panicked. Mark suggested calling the police and trying to get a restraining order, but she'd convinced him that they should go through academic channels first. If she'd had any idea how devastating even that would be for Seth, she never would have agreed. Afterward, Mark assured her that Seth's suicide attempt had been driven by mental instability and proved that seeking constraints on him for their own protection had been the wise course. If Mark had been lying about Seth all along, the effect of those accusations on the young man must have been doubly devastating. If only she'd known his tragic story beforehand. She'd still like to help Seth, still like to try to make it up to him in some small way, but he hasn't answered her letter, and she has to respect his desire to keep his distance.

So many questions: Did Mark lie about Seth, about Nico, about both? Did he imagine them to be threats? Has she missed signs that Mark is unstable, cold-blooded, or dishonest? The thought of trying to figure it all out is crushing. What's worse, there are no *good* answers here, no explanation that doesn't threaten the life she's always thought they had and counted on forever.

◆ ◆ ◆

Walking toward the house, Catherine sees Mark in the window, the warm yellow light behind him. Not long ago, that sight would have made Catherine happy, maybe even—it shames her to admit—more than a little smug. They were, after all, Catherine and Mark, the charmed couple, successful, attractive, made for each other. How sad that now her instinctive reaction is to slip away.

He's waiting when she opens the door. "Thank God you're all right! Where have you been?"

"I kayaked to Mozia to think." She continues her grudging list, recited like the entries on a police blotter. "Came back—I guess you didn't see me. Picked up the car. Spent the rest of the day in Marsala." Catherine sits at the table, and Mark joins her. He looks better than he did this morning. "You shaved," she says.

"For you." He covers her hand with his, a gesture she once found comforting and endearing. Right now it feels confining, but she leaves her hand there. This is still Mark.

Her desire for this to be the same familiar Mark softens her. "I'm sorry if I worried you. I needed some time alone."

"I understand. Can I get you tea or coffee? Or wine?"

"Sure. Tea. Let me help."

In the kitchen together, they are as awkward as strangers. When they return to the table, Catherine leans back in her seat, holding her cup with both hands.

"I know you must have questions, Cath. But before you say anything, let me apologize again. Not just for this morning. I was awful to you today, and I can only blame it on the stress I've been under. I will get a grip, I promise. But also . . . for lying to you. I'd give anything if I could go back and undo that one stupid lie."

"Was it only one?" Catherine places her cup on the table, one hand flat beside it.

"I know what you're saying. I kept lying about it. But honest to God, Cath, it was because I didn't know how to stop it without looking like a complete ass. Or worse." He slides his hand across the table, closer to hers. "You have to believe me."

"I don't think you do know what I'm saying. I *do* believe you couldn't find a way to back off that story of not seeing Nico. But . . ." She pauses, placing her hand over Mark's. His warm fist twitches slightly under hers. "Did you lie about Seth following you?" His hand tenses, but she maintains her gentle hold.

"What the—? I don't know what this has to do with anything, but no, of course not."

"It has everything to do with what you said today. Did you lie when you said Nico is stalking you?"

Mark withdraws his hand and moves to clasp Catherine's in both of his, but she withdraws hers, dropping them into her lap. He pulls back like a scolded child.

"Look at me. Look at what I was like this morning. I'm a wreck. I don't sleep. I think about this night and day. This has been going on for weeks. I'm telling you the truth."

"I want to believe you. But you keep telling only as much 'truth' as you feel you need to."

"Why would I say he was after me if he wasn't? You're crazy about him, and this pits me against him. Why would I do that?"

"Because you did it before with Seth, and you won."

Mark shifts in his seat as if he'd like to get up but knows he shouldn't. "I don't know what you're talking about." His voice is sharp, and he takes a breath before he continues, his tone softer, almost wistful. "Cath, all that matters is you and me. That's all I care about."

"Oh, please! I'm not a starry-eyed teenager. Do you think I expect or want you to care about nothing but us?"

"OK, but you are the *most* important thing to me."

"More important than being some kind of . . . of . . . real estate big shot?"

"Come on!" Mark's voice rises. "Since when is wanting to be successful at your chosen career wanting to be a big shot?"

"You know what? I think you say I'm all you care about because you want to make me feel I should have no interests but you."

"I can't even follow this anymore."

"*You* can't follow *me*? My head is spinning from all your stories. You'll say anything to get your way."

Mark gets up. He paces, his fear so frank that part of Catherine longs to comfort him. "Look, Cath, you make everything sound so black and white. But it's not that simple."

"I'd say this is anything but simple. But at least the basic facts—what actually happened—that should be something we can nail down with a little work." The bitterness and sarcasm of her words shock her, and she shakes off a pang of guilt.

"Look. I don't know. Maybe I made a mistake about Seth."

"How can you—what does 'maybe' mean? If you don't know, who does?"

"OK. OK. I . . . he didn't stalk me. You're right."

She looks away, studying a small tuft of lint snagged in the rough edge of one of the floorboards. She needs this not to be happening. "I wanted so much to be wrong about that. Even though I knew I wasn't. But it wasn't a mistake, Mark. It was a lie. You lied about Seth."

"I was worried about your safety. And about us, Cath. I thought you might be getting too close to Seth."

So this is what it's like to see all you have believed in and valued for a decade falling apart.

Mark sinks back into his chair, deflated, as if that last confession had been a revelation even to him, and voicing it had required more energy than he could afford. "I can't even begin to describe the guilt I feel about Seth. And I know this sounds crazy, but sometimes I think Nico knows what I did. And he's tormenting me for it. It's like we're locked in a fight for you. And I'm flat-out terrified he's winning."

◆ ◆ ◆

They'd slept perhaps three hours between them last night, and walking into the studio, Mark looks it. No doubt she does too. Tossing and turning is miserable enough without pretending not to notice the other person in your bed is doing the same thing. She knows she hadn't wanted any predawn talk about the crumbling life they're living, and she suspects Mark had felt the same way.

Mark sits next to Catherine. He takes a brush from the closest jar and examines it. "New kind?"

"Made in Italy. I like them a lot."

Catherine picks a few brushes from another jar. "These are a little different."

They labor to make small talk, stumbling over words and, after long silences, choosing the same moments to speak. Mark says, "I haven't felt this awkward with you since the night we met."

"It's no fun, is it?"

"Just don't shut me out." Mark arranges four paintbrushes into a square on the table. He removes one and uses it to coax the remaining three into a perfect triangle.

"Every time we talk about it, things get worse, not better."

"Maybe we should get away from here for a break. Take that ferry to Tunisia for a week or two. It would be someplace completely new and different."

"I'd like that. But . . . doing it now feels like running away. And this . . . Macri was supposed to be the break we needed. Right now, I need to be comfortable in my own mind that I understand what happened. Get back my confidence in you. If that's possible."

"Cath, you know me. Better than anyone. Nothing has changed. Sure, a lot of doubt has crept in because of this . . . this situation."

"Were there other times you made things up? To keep me from doing something you didn't want me to do?"

"No. The one and only time was with Seth."

"Not that time three years ago when I was going to spend the summer in Santa Fe working in Tina's studio? You told me she'd come on to you at the party, and I didn't go."

"No! Absolutely not." He grabs the brushes from the table and holds them in his fist.

"What about Scott? You stopped inviting him over because you said he'd done something inappropriate at work. But that was right after I joked about how good-looking he was. Was that jealousy too?"

"Scott routinely came back from lunch completely drunk and then behaved like a total ass. I didn't want him around anymore. You're blowing this thing way out of proportion."

Catherine looks Mark in the eye, trying to read what she sees there. Is the anger coming from him, or is it her own reflected back?

Mark checks his watch. He throws the brushes onto the table. "I have to get out of here for a while. Let's talk later."

"I'll be right here. But please, Mark, when you come back, come back ready to tell me the truth."

THIRTY-THREE

MARK

Mark drives into the parking lot, relieved to see only Paola's car remaining, baking in the late afternoon sun. Otherwise, he surely would have changed his mind. Because this is crazy. But he's desperate. He keeps reminding himself that no one ever has to know. He touches his shirt, feeling underneath it the *corna* he's taken to wearing the last few days. Entering the building, Mark finds Paola, keys in hand and about to switch out the lights.

"Signor Lindquist. In one more minute, you would have missed me. Let me get you your mail."

"Wait, Paola. Do you have a few minutes? There's something I was hoping you might help me with. Something personal."

Mark has received less-thorough appraisals in a doctor's office. With a few swift sweeps, Paola checks his eyes, his skin, his frame—several pounds thinner than it was when she saw him last—and nods her head once. "It is your—illness? This is why you need my help?"

"It's not really an illness, Paola. I was not—not fully honest with you. There is someone—someone bad—who is following me. He—he's everywhere, and I can't even sleep. I—"

"This does not surprise me. In my *villaggio*, and in many all over Italy, we know a bad person in your life can make you sick. This person, if he has the magic, he can place the evil eye on you and can do terrible things—visiting you in your bed when you try to sleep, giving you many frights and destroying your healthiness."

Mark leans back against the wall. "I don't know what to do. I was hoping—I mean, you seemed to know something of this?"

"I can take you to someone who is skilled in the arts you need. Some call such people *strega*, some say *maga*—there are other names. She can help you."

Mark nods. This is what he wanted, yet he's having trouble keeping second thoughts at bay. "I hope—It's very important that this talk we are having, that it stay between you and me only."

"Of course! You may trust me totally."

"I do. Thank you. Can we go right now?"

"Signor Lindquist, I am sorry, but tonight I—" She looks into his eyes and sighs. "OK. Tonight."

Leaving their cars behind in a small pull-off area on the edge of a hilly village, Paola and Mark walk through the narrow, winding streets of a place as old and unchanged as Erice, but which is, in its plainness and scale, far less charming. As best he can tell, this place with no name—when he had asked, Paola had said it was "difficult to explain"—has one narrow main street with a handful of narrower side branches. He again has the sense of returning to the Middle Ages, but unlike Erice, where it had felt like a magical gift, here it seems more like a somber penance.

At the end of a tiny street, Paola stops in front of a wooden door covered with sprigs of dried herbs, bundled with cord and hanging from rusty nails. On the wall directly next to the door is a shallow wooden box with a glass door. Inside, a painting of a Madonna, pink-cheeked and wearing a crown of small gold stars, keeps a cheerless eye on any and all visitors. A white candle in a crystal jar burns to her left, while to her right a matching jar holds a tidy bouquet of fresh flowers. Paola signals Mark to stop a few feet back before she knocks. An elderly woman, her olive skin pleated and leathered from what must have been decades working in the fields, answers. Dressed in black, the woman smiles when she recognizes Paola who, he surmises, is explaining his plight. The woman turns her head sharply toward Mark, narrowing one eye as she looks him over. She fires off three or four questions to Paola, and when she has her answers, she nods and turns to go back inside.

Mark follows Paola through the door, stopping at the sound and feel of grit under his feet. "Salt," Paola explains. "To keep away the bad luck that might come in with visitors." The woman disappears into the next room.

"Flavia will be right back." Paola stands, her hands together at her waist, like a child in the principal's office.

Mark looks around the busy space. In one corner of the room a tiny window admits little light, since layers of red-and-black lace cover the glass and form a backdrop for three small tables. One table is a jumble of what he takes to be family photos, a single candle burning in front of the grouping, and a *corna* charm hanging over each frame. On the second table sit half a dozen jars containing bunches of fresh herbs. A head of garlic, three eggs, pins of varying lengths, spools of thread, an eyedropper, small glass bowls, and cruets of rich green olive oil and water vie for space with a collection of unlit black candles. The third table holds a lineup of very small dolls, featureless and made of plain beige cloth, along with scissors, a sharp knife, and a pile of sea shells.

Mark can't even begin to take in the variety of icons hanging on the walls. Many are familiar, but others do not look as if they'd be at home in a church. He turns when Flavia enters the room carrying a folded white sheet and a small floral demitasse cup. She spreads the sheet out on the couch, then motions that Mark is to lie down and lift his shirt.

Flavia takes the cup, rubs the edge with garlic and a drop of oil, and presses it, rim down, over Mark's navel. He looks at Paola, who says, "She is testing for the worms."

"Worms! I—"

"The worms can be real or can be the black magic in your body from the bad person. Please wait. If the cup sticks to you, you have worms."

Flavia pushes the cup, and it does not move. She nods.

"She will now rid you of the worms."

At Paola's words, Mark feels the blood drain from his face. "I'm not sure about this, Paola. How?"

"Very simple and quick."

Flavia returns from the altar with another small bowl filled with oil. She dips her thumb into the oil and makes tiny crosses, redipping her thumb when needed, all over Mark's abdomen.

"This should work in one day, maybe two, but you must also wear the charm Flavia will give you."

"I am already wearing the charm you gave me, Paola."

"Yes, that is good to keep away the evil eye, but this new one—*la cimaruta*—this is a very powerful one and protects you against any magic used against you."

Mark sits up, and Flavia hands him a small tin charm. It resembles branching coral, but at the end of each branch is a symbol—a dagger, a half-moon, a key, a rooster's head. There are more, but Mark looks up as Flavia takes it and, reaching around his neck, slips it onto the chain he already wears. She says something to Paola while waving her index finger at Mark.

"She says never take this off for one moment. Not for the shower or to sleep or anything at all."

169

"OK. Is there more we can do?"

Paola speaks to Flavia, then turns to Mark. "Come back with a picture of the bad person. A photo is best, but make a drawing if you have nothing else. And she will tell you how to do the banishing magic."

Only after he thanks Flavia—and pays her—thanks Paola, and returns to his car does he allow himself to think about what he's just done. His shame at sinking to such utter nonsense is profound, but his fear is sharp—fear that others will find out, and fear that none of this will work.

THIRTY-FOUR

CATHERINE

It's late in the afternoon when Mark returns. With the low sun behind him in the doorway, he's more a set of shadows and glares than anything like a solid human being. But Catherine would know his walk anywhere. She remembers when their relationship was new and they'd meet at the end of the day outside the subway stop to go home together. Even in the crowded streets, she always smiled at the sight of his familiar step. Now, she presses her lips together, fearful that he's come prepared to be less than truthful again. Or even worse, that the truth he tells will be something she doesn't want to know.

Mark sighs as he sits on a stool facing Catherine. She stops her work and folds her hands on the table, giving him her full attention. When Mark speaks, he simply picks up the conversation where it left off—no greeting, no preamble, but no anger either.

"I lied about seeing Nico because I was jealous of the time you spent with him. It's like you're infatuated with him. It was stupid, and I acted on an impulse—a bad one. But there I was, living with the guilt of what I did to Seth. And to you. When I walked in here that day to see Nico . . . looking just like Seth . . . it was beyond creepy. It rattled me."

"So you're saying at first, you imagined a Nico who looked like Seth. OK. And then what? You gave that one up when you saw the real one? Or did Nico change? Did he stay looking like Seth only long enough to give you an excuse for acting like a jerk? Help me understand here."

"Change? He didn't change."

"You can do better than this. Why don't you take a minute to dream up something more plausible? I'll wait."

"Meaning what?"

"Oh, please! If Nico and Seth looked even a little bit alike—"

"But—I mean, sure, Nico has a baby face. But it's Seth's face."

Catherine stands and picks up a pile of sketch pads. She puts one on the table in front of Mark, flipping through sketch after sketch, watercolor after watercolor, all of Nico. "Look. Show me where you see Seth's features anywhere in that face."

Mark leans away from the pad, as if afraid he might touch it by accident. He's beginning to understand something. That day in the Uffizi, looking up into the face of the *Spinario*, the face Catherine had said looked so much like Nico—he'd panicked, feeling something was terribly wrong. Because he hadn't seen anything of Nico in that face. Later, he'd put it out of his mind, convincing himself that Catherine's perception had grown out of her unhealthy preoccupation with the boy. But now he sees she was right. The boy in these sketches could easily, in ten or so years, look just like the face on that statue. But then who is he seeing? How could it be that when he and Catherine together looked right at the boy in the barn, they saw such different faces? "That's what you think Nico looks like? Curly dark hair? And that broad face? Because that is not the Nico I've seen. Not even close."

Catherine puts her hands over her ears. "Stop!"

"Listen to me!" He's shouting now. "The Nico I've seen has straight blond hair. And very fine features. A long, slender face. He looks just like Seth."

"Which you're mentioning for the first time now?"

"Why would I mention what he looked like? Why would I ever even consider the crazy idea that we weren't seeing the same thing? You seem so sure that I'm lying or wrong, but maybe it's you. I don't understand what's going on here any more than you do."

"Really? Now I'm supposed to feel sorry for poor, befuddled, innocent you? As stories go, Mark, this one's not terribly good."

◆　◆　◆

The studio is lonely without Nico. Working from memory, Catherine is finishing up a clay model of the boy when Mark walks in. In his suit and tie, carrying his black-leather portfolio, he looks sharp and put together. Catherine could almost let herself forget how disheveled and—well, if she's honest with herself—how frightening he's looked recently. That "almost," though, that's a miss as good as a mile. With a twinge of sadness, she realizes she doesn't know what he's doing today.

"If I'm not interrupting, is there a surface I can use? To show you something?"

Catherine walks to a different table, and Mark follows. She piles up the scatter of sketches there and gestures to the cleared area.

Mark unzips the case. "I'm going to Palermo. Overnight because I have meetings tonight and tomorrow."

"OK."

"I hope that by tomorrow afternoon, these plans . . ." He places his hands on top of the large white sheets of paper. ". . . will be ready to show to the office in New York. This could be huge for us, Cath. And I mean more than financially. We'd be coming back to Italy whenever we wanted."

"We're here now."

"Yes." Mark's tone is controlled and calm. "But I need to go back to New York in a few weeks at most. Of course, we'll pay Giulia for the full time we rented. I'm assuming you're coming back with me."

When Catherine doesn't answer, Mark arranges the plans on the desk. There are six pairs, each with a "before" drawing of a rural property with traditional buildings and a more modernized "after." Some limit changes to a bit of sprucing up, perhaps with an added parking area and an outdoor terrace or two. Others are more elaborate and include new architectural features such as pillars, gates, verandas, and swimming pools. Catherine recognizes Roberto's place in Riposto. Most of the lemon grove remains, but some of it has given way to tourist conveniences. Of the remaining pairs of drawings, four are not familiar to Catherine, but the fifth is Giulia's place.

Catherine looks up at Mark. "Giulia?"

"She hasn't said yes yet."

She pushes the drawings aside. "I don't want to see these. You know how I feel about ruining these places."

"I'm not—" He takes a deep breath, then tightens his lips as if he's promised himself he won't lose control. "I've been very respectful of the traditional architecture—and the natural characteristics—of each place. I actually love architecture, as I pretty much think you know. I want to preserve these places. They've been in their families forever, and people want to do what they can to keep them. This is the best way I can think of. But nothing can stay unchanged forever, Catherine. You have to look to the future, not just the past."

"You talked to Giulia without ever telling me."

"For God's sake, it's work, Catherine." He raises his arms, palms up—a large, questioning gesture that professes innocence and exasperation at the same time. "It's not like I was hiding it."

Catherine returns to her clay, prodding and poking with more heat than usual. Neither of them speaks for a full minute.

Mark shuffles his weight from one leg to another and checks his watch. "Are you pretending I'm not here?"

"You'll be back when?"

"Perfect! Great way to address reality. But then, that hasn't been your strong suit lately, has it? It might interfere with your Sicilian-farm-girl fantasy." He gathers up his plans and puts them away. "I'll be back tomorrow night, probably late. I hope you can get it together and think about this while I'm gone. It's not what you're making it out to be. If you open up your mind, you'll see that it helps people who—"

"Have a safe trip."

Catherine senses Mark looking at her for a long time but ignores him.

"All right." Mark turns to leave, then stops and speaks over his shoulder. "Maybe we can talk when you're a little more rational." He walks out.

High up in the olive grove, Catherine looks down toward the shoreline, today stolen from view by the dense morning fog. The somber mist reaches inland, translucent clouds of it tangled in the gnarled trees, smearing silvery leaves into ghostly blobs. Ancient branches bend and twist like desperate arms beseeching the sky for sun. Catherine remembers thinking when they first arrived that it was always sunny here. It isn't, but even in this gray and dreary weather, there's a special kind of beauty. In the distance, a dark figure stands in Catherine's path, and she hesitates until she recognizes Assunta.

Catherine walks to meet Assunta, who remains in place, leaning on her walking stick. "Such an unusual morning. I couldn't resist coming here."

"Every morning, I come here to look at these trees. Most times, my only companion is my walking stick. And the ghosts."

"Ghosts?"

"Of my husband, my father, his father, and many fathers before. They all one time work these trees. It is like they speak to me here. But today, I have you for a companion too." Assunta takes Catherine's arm, and they walk along together, Assunta leaning on Catherine for balance when the ground grows rough.

"I'm honored to be in such company. You know, I think maybe I can hear them too."

"Maybe you hear them because they are, I think, sad."

"Why is that?"

"Giulia—maybe she will have to sell our land."

The words strike Catherine like a slap.

"She does not wish this, but her two brothers . . . em . . . they also—all together with Giulia, yes?—they own this farm. And she thinks they will like too much the sound of the money."

"Do you mean sell to—" Catherine stops, unsure of how much Assunta knows of Mark's plans. She feels guilty even though it looks like she was the last to know. "Mark—he only told me yesterday, and I—"

"I know this idea, it is not from you. I do not understand too much about it, but Giulia says some men, they have money and want to buy part of our home. They will build a fancy new place with more rooms, and Giulia and I will have many guests."

"Does it make you sad too?"

"I'm an old lady whose heart is here. On this land."

"But, Assunta, if it does happen, surely you will stay here and live. Like now."

Assunta bunches the fingertips of her right hand and points them to the sky, shaking her hand up and down. "Never the same. I do not like people to come here who like only money and want swimming pools and fancy rooms." She shrugs. "I know. Everything changes, but this"—and she sweeps with her arm to take in the olive grove—"I hope that she never change."

Was that a slip of the tongue, or does Assunta think of the farm as a person? Catherine pulls a supple olive branch toward her and wipes the moisture from one of the olives. "Why don't the birds eat these?"

"They learn they are very, very bitter. More bitter than anything. Try if you like."

"That's OK." Catherine laughs. "I believe you."

"This bitterness—it comes from our history. You know some of this history, yes, Catherine?"

"I'm not sure which part you mean. I've learned so much since I've been here, but—"

"I mean the children—the murdered children from long ago. There are so many, and they are all around us." She places a shaky hand onto Catherine's arm. Catherine's heart races. "The bitter, it is their sadness. All they want, these babies, is for someone to love them. They want—" Assunta becomes flustered. "*La possibilità*—how do you say this?"

"The chance."

"Yes. The chance to grow up. Like the olives. Bitter now, but when you take them and treat them just the right way—the way we have done in Sicilia for the centuries—they become sweet."

"I've never heard any of this."

"Local people—we don't like to say because it sounds crazy a little bit. But some of us know. Our salt—we have been blessed with this for so long—this comes from the tears of these children." Assunta looks Catherine in the eye, and Catherine returns her gaze, exhilarated and at the same time terrified. "This place is very special. Like no other. Do you understand, Catarina, what I tell you?"

Catherine's heart skips a beat at *Catarina*. "I think I do."

"When one of these children chooses somebody—only special people can understand. But I think from the first day we meet—I think you are going to be one of them."

◆ ◆ ◆

Catherine sits on the small wooden porch pretending to read. It's the first time Nico has come to the house, and she's too excited to focus. He sits cross-legged on the weathered floorboards, staring out to sea. She hopes no splinters will hurt the tender undersides of his thighs.

She's thinking about finding some children's books at the library, something she can read aloud to Nico, when she hears Mark approaching. She looks at Nico. Will he stay? Before she speaks, Nico gives one shake of his head and steps off the porch, slipping behind a dense pink oleander shrub bristling with bees.

When Mark opens the door and steps onto the porch, there is no sign that Catherine has not been alone. He sits next to her and raises his coffee cup as if in salute. "Morning."

"Hi. What time did you get in last night? I didn't hear you." Why did she say that? Is this what they've come to—lying to one another as easily as not?

"After midnight. How's everything here?"

"Fine. And your trip?"

"Fine."

They sit, in almost pure silence, their few brief bits of conversation addressing a flickering warning light on the car dashboard and a creaking shutter on one of the bedroom windows. Neither has said a word for quite some time when Catherine speaks.

"I talked to Assunta yesterday."

"Oh?"

She describes the conversation, and Mark's face goes from guarded when she speaks about the potential sale to impatient when she reaches the part about the Phoenician children. "So maybe there's something to this idea that you are seeing a different child. If they're everywhere here, maybe it isn't Nico at all. Maybe another child has chosen to be visible to you."

"And why would this second child be doing that?" Mark sounds bored, and Catherine's resolve to remain friendly and nonconfrontational is washing away.

"Because he needs us too."

"For God's sake, Catherine, now you think we need to adopt two dead boys?"

"But think about what Assunta said! It all fits. I—"

"I don't know what you heard—or think you heard—Assunta say, but we aren't being courted by two dead Phoenician kids. Nothing you told me about what she said included anything specific. It seems to me you took the philosophical musings of a woman whose English is not all that great to begin with and heard what you wanted to hear." He pauses and moves his chair a little closer to Catherine, facing her more. He leans in and his voice softens, becomes solicitous. "You need to get away, Catherine. This place—it's so insular, like you're in exile from the real world. Two days away made such a difference for me. I know it would help you too."

"Help me what, Mark? Forget everything I've seen and heard from Nico? That won't happen."

"It might help you to focus on us. We're falling apart here. That alone is reason enough to leave. I want to go back to New York—two, three weeks from now tops. And I don't want to go back without you. We can fix things. I know it."

"I still care about you too. But how do I reconcile that with how much I dislike your plan? The one that might force Giulia's hand. And I don't want to go back to New . . . no, that's not true. It's not what I *don't* want to do. It's that I *want* to stay here, with you. I need you to consider that possibility."

"How can I when there is no life for us here, Catherine?"

"Life would be different; it's true. The thing is, I think it would be better if you would give it half a chance."

"I'll say the same to you: come back with me, give it a try. If it doesn't work out . . ."

"I'd like to go back to New York for a while. Seth never wrote me, and I'd still like to make things right with him, especially knowing what I know now."

"Oh, jeez, sure. Spread your new earth-mother wealth. Keep a charity case on each continent."

"That wasn't necessary, Mark. Not if you're serious about trying to find an answer to all this."

"You're right. I'm a little strung out right now."

"I know. Me too. I don't know how I can leave, and I don't know how I can stay without you either. It's an impossible situation."

Mark turns toward a rustle in the oleanders. "What was that?"

"That sound? Probably some birds. There were a bunch in there before." Lying gets a little easier each time.

Cleaning up her table, Catherine tries to remember if there are any leftovers in the fridge. The past several days, for whatever reasons—or excuses—she and Mark haven't managed a meal together once. Tonight he has a working dinner in Palermo with some colleagues. She's tempted to go to their usual place in Marsala, but she fears finding Mark there too, alone. Then she'll know that the "working dinner" was a lie to avoid her.

"*Buonasera!*" Catherine looks up at the sound of a voice from the doorway. It's Giulia, carrying a crockery bowl covered with a dish towel. "I made some *arancini*, and I know you like them. Three kinds—with peas, with mozzarella, and with pistachio. For your dinner."

"Sometimes I think you know what I want before I do." Catherine peeks under the dish towel at three rows of pudgy-bottomed rice balls. They come to pixieish peaks and wear deep-fried coats of crispy bread crumbs. "They look perfect!"

"I will teach you these later in the week. Very easy." Giulia walks around the studio, examining things with a level of interest that suggests she's stalling.

"Catherine," she says, "I have something to ask."

"Sit down, Giulia. In the rocking chair. Which has been so wonderful out here, by the way. Thank you again."

"It was nothing." Giulia sits. She clasps and unclasps her fingers as if no position is quite comfortable. "My question, though—is big. I want to know if—maybe—you and Mark would think about buying this place."

Catherine isn't sure what she was expecting, but this wasn't it. "This place, meaning?"

"The whole place. Both houses, the barn, the olives, all of it."

"But, Giulia—"

"Change is coming. All we ask, my mother and I, is to live here until we go. We can work out together a way to do this that is good for everybody. If you and Mark can make a good offer, I know I can talk to my brothers to take it, and they will."

"I don't know what to say."

"It must be before Mark's investors make a bigger offer because then I must tell my brothers. These investors—they will not love the place the way I know you and Mark will love it."

"I do love it. And I'm so embarrassed that Mark is behaving the way he is."

"Mark is a good man. He must do these things for his work. But once he lives here, it will be different. I can still work the olives and help you to hire more workers. And you can do your art here. I would be very happy. You and Mark would be very happy. *Everyone* would be happy. Do you understand what I am saying to you?"

"That Assunta would be happy?"

"Yes, Assunta too. But . . ."

Catherine hesitates, then says, "Nico?"

"*Mamma* and I, we always knew you would understand."

The next afternoon in the studio, Catherine works as Nico sits on the floor nearby. She's pretty sure Mark's at a meeting—was it in Trapani? A few short months ago, they always knew each other's plans, although now she can't help wondering how often Mark was being straight with her. When she hears him approaching, she looks to Nico, who slips into the shadows toward the east end of the barn.

"Getting a lot done?" Mark puts his suit jacket over the back of a stool and sits.

"Surprisingly so. You?"

"The meeting went well. I guess you were out for a walk when I left today."

Catherine wipes her hands on a damp cloth. "In the olive grove again. Those trees have more personality than a lot of people I know. I think I'll try some sculptures of them tomorrow, or at least of some branches."

"Nice. The olive branch—the official peace offering. Accepted everywhere."

"Hadn't thought of that. I've been thinking about them on a less metaphorical level."

Mark gets up and walks over to another table, hands in pockets. "I haven't seen much of your sketch work lately. I miss that."

"Maybe this evening we can go through some together."

"Sure."

Catherine looks away from Mark's "You and I both know we won't" expression. "Giulia came by yesterday. I tried to wait up to tell you."

"Oh. Anything wrong?"

"She wanted to ask us something." She rushes to finish, sprinting to get through what Mark's face tells her is a swiftly closing door. "It would be a wonderful chance for us. To start over."

"Start over here with Nico, you mean."

"We could put the past behind us. All of it—Seth, what's been happening here between us. It would be a fresh beginning."

"I've said it all before. I can't trap myself here, in a place I don't want to be, and with no end to this Nico thing. I need to get away, not move here. Don't you see that?"

"I don't. I don't know what you're trying to escape."

"Me? You're the one trying to escape. You can't face your life back in New York. You want to hide here, you want me to hide with you, and you want me to share in your joy about Nico. When he—or some other phantom child—wants to harm me. And you don't seem to care about that at all."

"You can't stop lying, can you?"

"Look. We're not getting anywhere." He reaches into his pocket and takes out a pen. Ripping a page from one of Catherine's sketch pads, he writes. "I'm going to go throw together some clothes and spend a few days in Trapani. At this hotel." He pockets the pen. "We both need some time to think alone."

"Fine. Go."

"I don't like saying this any more than you're going to like hearing it, but I'm afraid it's coming down to a choice—Nico or me."

"Or maybe you're the one who has to choose."

"There is no choice for me. I cannot and will not stay where I'm not safe."

Catherine sits down in the rocking chair, head in her hands. "How did we get here, Mark? I thought we'd always be happy. Each other's biggest ally. Now, I don't even know you." She whispers, "Or trust you."

"I'm the same guy, Catherine. Come back home. Break the stranglehold this place has on you and things will look just the way they used to." Mark looks down at the floor, jingling the car keys in his pocket. "I didn't want to mention this before because it's so—it sounds—I'd think it was unhinged if someone else said it. But it's more than a threat I'm worried about with Nico—or whoever the hell he is. He actually assaulted me."

"Oh, for God's sake, Mark. How far will you go with this?"

In two strides, Mark is at Catherine's chair. He leans in over her, looking straight into her eyes. "It was the middle of the night. He got on top of me and kept touching my face. He painted my face with blood. With blood, Catherine! I thought I would lose my fucking mind. It was horrifying. I've never been that scared. Not even close."

"And where was I?"

Mark paces. "Right there. Asleep."

"Why didn't I see any blood on you or our bed or the floor—or anywhere? Come on, Mark, it was a guilty nightmare. If you aren't making it all up on the spot."

"What can I do to make you believe me? What would make you stop being so angry and listen to me?"

"The only thing that would help me now is if I never have to hear you or any of your disgusting lies again."

Mark grabs his jacket. "Your concern is touching. I'll be back in three or four days."

Catherine refuses to watch Mark leave. Let him be dramatic. Let him go. The car door slams, the engine starts, and a piercing squeal fades down the driveway, leaving a harsh silence behind.

A rustling sound from the back corner breaks the stillness as Nico steps out of the shadows. Approaching Catherine, he climbs into her lap, so cautious and gentle as to be almost ethereal, and settles there, head on her shoulder, body a fetal curl. Catherine lays a tentative hand on the back of his head, and when he does not object, she wraps her other arm around him. Stroking his hair, she rocks him like an infant. "I will always love you, Nico." Nico looks up into her face, and Catherine's heart fills with tenderness and uncomplicated contentment as he touches her cheek and smiles.

THIRTY-FIVE

MARK

Sitting on the hard ground in the windy tophet, Mark checks his watch. Five minutes until midnight. He's pretty sure he just said that out loud. He's been doing that a lot the past three days, not that anyone's been around who could possibly care. Unless that kid cares. *He's* been around, although not this evening, at least so far.

Placing the black candle on the uneven dirt in front of him, Mark worries and works it into a stable position and takes the sketch of Nico from his pocket. He had watched Flavia fold it, each move precise, and sew it closed with a smothering of meticulous small crosses. He'd done as she instructed and carried it with him for two days, periodically chanting the words she'd taught him, which, Paola assured him, boil down to "Get lost." He laughs but stops as the gusty wind blows the chilling sound of quavering echoes to his ears. The whole thing is ludicrous, and he ought to just stop now, but . . .

From a white plastic bag, Mark takes a bowl, a bottle of water, and a jar filled with a golden liquid Flavia had said was the best for this kind of thing. What kind is that? Laughing again, something he's quite certain Flavia would frown upon, he places the bowl next to the candle and pours in the water. When it settles, he adds the liquid almost drop by drop, letting it form a fat layer on the water's surface. Hey, this will make a great topic of conversation the next time Richard and Simone give a party. Oh yeah. Simone was right. He's so lucky to get to experience this firsthand.

He looks up at the sound of a twig cracking and holds still. It had to be the wind. This dismal island is hardly a hot spot for the locals. He hesitates. The next step will leave him unable to hear or see anything around him—not that there's anything but this blasted wind. Taking a thin plastic tarp from the bag, he drapes it over himself, the candle, and the bowl, pulling a portion of it under himself and sitting on it. This takes an exasperating amount of work, since the wind appears bent on taking the tarp sailing. Using sand and rocks—and probably pieces of precious Phoenician pottery, Catherine, so how do you like that? Meet your expectations of Mark as the Philistine?—he at last secures the tarp to his satisfaction. Flavia had specified two companions holding a dark blanket over his head, but, hey, a guy can only do what he can do. Imagine if Flavia knew he wasn't even sure this cemetery was the kid's home?

In the pitch black of the enclosure, Mark feels for the candle and the matches. The racket of the tarp in the wind is pissing him off now, but he's almost done. He lights the candle, nearly burning his fingers, and touches a corner of the sketch to the flame. It flares, and he lifts the photo and moves it toward the bowl. He pauses. Maybe it's not too late to stop and retain some shreds of self-respect. But he's too far gone for that. All that's left now is to repeat the chant three times and make sure the picture burns to ash, so he shrugs. Flavia had warned twice that if it burned partway, if the slightest bits were left, his situation could get much worse. He begins the chant and drops the photo into the bowl. The liquid on the surface bursts into a hot green flame, and when Mark jerks away, the wind frees a corner of the tarp, which dips into the bowl, igniting. Mark reaches forward, hoping to stop it, but he hits the bowl, splashing flaming liquid onto the tarp. The flame twists its way along the tarp, connecting the dots of splashed golden liquid, and in moments, he's in a burning cocoon that clings to him, hot and tenacious, even when he stands. The wind pushes the thin plastic against him, and as he struggles to free himself, the melting plastic sticks in agonizing patches to his bare skin while the fumes burn his throat and lungs. When he finally escapes, the fire out, he bends, hands on his knees, breath harsh, eyes tearing.

What a fuckup. He couldn't even do this right—a stupid, senseless ritual probably dreamed up in the year 1300 by some toothless village idiot. He's got to get out of here. He's got to get himself straightened out back home. He can come back for Catherine later.

THIRTY-SIX

CATHERINE

Surrounded by a tangle of clay olive branches, Catherine adjusts the armature for a small tree, trying for the perfect twist to the limbs. The right warp and curve is critical to capturing the grace and charm of these old souls. Every few minutes she looks up to see if Nico is here, but he never is. He hasn't been back since the afternoon he sat on her lap, the afternoon Mark left almost four days ago. Did Nico decide she'd gone too far? Or maybe that was a farewell hug he'd given her. It's too sad to think that, even for a minute.

It's just as sad to think she might lose Mark. This could be—should be—such a happy time for all three of them. It would break her heart to leave Nico now. At the same time, the thought that she owes Mark a chance haunts her, a chance, as he said, on their home territory. She prides herself on being sensible and observant. You can't be an artist without being a good observer. So she would have noticed at some time in ten years if Mark had been a liar, wouldn't she? Is he right—that she's in the thrall of this magical place, and once she gets away, she'll see Mark and Nico more clearly? But who's to say it isn't the other way around? That in New York, she's under the spell of Mark, and only here has been able to see the truth. Then again, it's possible that her failure to detect what was coming with Seth proves she's not the sharp observer she likes to think she is.

Catherine looks up at soft footfalls approaching the barn. There are too many for it to be Nico. It must be several people, adults from the sound. They are speaking Italian, sober and subdued, and she can make out enough as they get closer to know it is Giulia and two men who seem to want Catherine.

Giulia enters first, followed by the men, their uniforms identifying them as municipal police. Nico! Something's happened to Nico. Let it not be that.

After brief introductions, one of the officers nods to Giulia. "Catherine, these gentlemen asked me to tell you why they have come today. I'm afraid the news is not so good. It is about Mark. He is in hospital now after these men found him."

"Found him?"

"They found him alone on Mozia in the tophet. They think he must have been there all the night before, maybe longer. He was in—how do you say this?—the shock? He has some serious burns. And he has not spoken to anyone."

"Burns? Why was he there, and what he was doing? And—he hasn't spoken at all?"

Giulia confers with the police. "No, he says not a single word to anyone. Not one word. No one knows why he was there. They found some things—some things people use for Sicilian magic near where they found him."

She drops onto her stool. "Magic? That's not Mark."

"The police, they want to know if you know why he would need this?"

Catherine shakes her head no.

"And—" Giulia hesitates.

"Giulia—what? Tell me."

"They found his car on the main island. And in it they found some letters to you from a man. Seth—"

"Seth! To me here? In Sicily?"

"Yes. And—these letters were wrapped in some herbs also used for the Sicilian magic to make a person—em—leave your life. The police want to know if this Seth is here and where they should look for him."

"I—I don't know. I didn't know anything about them. The letters, I mean." She covers her face with her hands. "I need to see Mark. I don't understand any of this."

"Catherine?"

Catherine looks up to see Sandra approaching. When had she come in? She notices Kenneth standing next to Giulia, baby Valeria in his arms and Claudio at his side. Had he been there all along? And Assunta at Giulia's other side. She's sure Assunta hadn't been there a few moments ago.

Sandra sits next to Catherine and puts an arm around her shoulders. "Giulia called us. She thought we might be a comfort to you. Kenneth and I will help you with everything—getting to see Mark, making sure he gets the right care, all of it."

Catherine can't think straight. Giulia must have called Sandra and Kenneth before she came to tell Catherine about Mark. That makes no sense.

"Catherine." Sandra's eyes are sympathetic, her voice soft. "We are all your family here. We will—all of us—all help you through this."

Before she can reply, a sensation of being watched seizes Catherine, one she has not experienced in a long time. Now, though, her deep unease comes not from fear of the unknown, but from the horror of what she is quite sure she does know. She turns, and there, in the shadows, is Nico. Without moving a muscle, he catches her eye, holds her gaze, and smiles.

THIRTY-SEVEN

April 2016—twenty-three years later

Catherine stands in the doorway, watching; her latest guests are due any moment. She notices that the sign is getting worn, the letters fading from their original blood red to a dusky rose. That will need attention. At the sound of tires on the dirt drive, half a dozen hens scatter, squawking their grievances.

Catherine smooths the front of her blouse, checking that it is clean and presentable before opening the door and greeting the young American couple. "Welcome to *Agriturismo di Caterina*. You must be Deirdre and Lawrence."

"Yes. Dee and Larry. And you are Catherine?"

"I am. This is my favorite moment—when my guests go from being names on an e-mail to flesh-and-blood people. Come in. Come to the desk, and let's get you settled."

Catherine opens the register to a page marked with a crimson ribbon. "If you would sign in, please. And fill in here." She points. "I'll need to see your passports. The Italian government requires it."

"Sure." Larry picks up a pen and writes.

"Would you like help with your bags?"

"That would be nice," says Dee.

"Nico!" A tall, almost-beautiful young man comes out from a back room in response to Catherine's call. "This is my son." His smile is warm and welcoming as he shakes hands with Dee and Larry. "You can always ask him if you need help with something. Right now, Nico, please get the bags for these nice people, and bring them to number three."

As Larry writes, Dee walks to a far wall and examines the framed photos there. "Oh. Is this Nico, here?" She points to a faded photo of a young boy.

Catherine joins her. "Yes. When we first met him." At the look of confusion on Dee's face, she adds, "He's adopted. This wall shows our cast of characters, you might say." She points to a photo. "Giulia is one of the owners of this place. And this is Assunta, Giulia's mother. She's ninety-four years old and as sharp as a tack. She loves to meet guests. And she has so many stories about the history of this place."

"That sounds wonderful," says Dee.

"Sometimes she and Giulia offer cooking lessons, if you and Larry are interested."

Dee points to a dozen photos in the wall grouping. "And who are all these people?"

"Oh, they're American expat families we've known over the years. Most of their children are so grown up now." She sighs.

As Catherine turns to go back to the desk, Larry says, "Done!"

"Now, let me explain our setup." Catherine glances at the passports and returns the documents to Larry and Dee. "We live in the rest of this big house—along with Giulia and Assunta—an extended family, you might say. I work in the barn out there. I'm an artist. And you're welcome to come by anytime and visit with me there. This room is a common area for our guests, and all the books, games, and maps here are for your use. Right now, the other three guesthouses are empty, but two are booked for the weekend." She points to the opposite wall. "You can borrow DVDs from that shelf if you like. We have no streaming here,

I'm afraid, but you do have Wi-Fi—most times—and the password is on your kitchen table. You'll also find a little plate of homemade Sicilian cookies there, from Giulia. They are Bones of the Dead, but don't let the name put you off. They're delicious dipped into your coffee. Or wine!"

"That's a beautiful painting." Larry points to a fiery-toned canvas, an abstract sunset over the lagoon. "Same artist as the one on the far wall?"

"Oh, yes. Seth. Everyone loves Seth's paintings. He was a student of mine back in New York. He's been an important influence for Nico growing up, what with my husband's problems—"

A clatter from a darkened corner of the room causes everyone to look. "Oh. That's Mark now. He must have dropped his book." She walks over to Mark, who is sitting, staring straight ahead, his face expressionless. Catherine picks up the book, its spine twisted from the fall, and puts it on the table next to his chair. "Mark doesn't speak. Or get around much." She crouches down and looks into Mark's eyes. "Do you, Mark? Now, can I get you something?" Mark does not respond in any way. Catherine smiles and stands up.

Joining Larry back at the desk, she adds in a quiet voice, "It's a very old health issue. Nothing you need to worry about. Generally, he stays in the main part of the house. But if he's here when you come to use the common room, don't feel you have to talk to him. He doesn't really—communicate."

"Oh, OK. I'll tell Dee. She's back over there looking at those photos." He raises his voice. "Hey, Dee? Hon?"

Dee comes to the desk, and Catherine busies herself finding the extra cottage key while Larry tells Dee about Mark. Neither appears too disturbed by the specter of Mark, glum and expressionless, rooted to his chair. Catherine does think, however, there will be a little discussion between Larry and Dee later.

"Catherine?" Dee looks curious. "Who was that little girl?"

"Little girl?"

Dee turns and points out the window next to the wall of photographs. "Out there. She was watching me, and when I caught her eye, she ran away."

"Really? I don't know."

"She was so cute."

Catherine smiles. "Maybe you'll see her again. For now, though, let's get you settled in. You must both be tired. Come, I'll take you to your cottage."

Catherine holds the door open as they step out into the sunshine. "It's just a short walk, and along the way, I'll tell you about your cottage, and you can tell me more about yourselves. Do you have any children of your own at home?"

AUTHOR'S NOTE

Macri is a fictional town. Aside from Macri itself, however, all the geography in this book is real. The submerged road to Mozia is not on most maps but is visible on satellite images such as those of Google Maps. The modern name for the island, which is privately owned by the Whitaker Foundation, is San Pantaleo, although Mozia and Mothia are in common use.

The tiny peek at the enormously long and complex history of Sicily I presented, from the Phoenician settlement to the long-standing salt industry, is genuine. There is not universal agreement that Phoenicians practiced ritual child sacrifice, but the evidence is strong, and recent analyses of the bones found in these children's cemeteries—which also include the bones of small animals—back up the belief.

Although Western Sicily, as I have tried to show, is wildly beautiful, it is decidedly not stuck in the shadowy dark ages. If you go to Sicily, you will find old beauty, wonderful food, vibrant cities, stunning ruins, and warm, friendly people—who are not witches.

Sicilian and familial magic is a subject of some controversy. Among believers, practices vary widely, and many are secret. They are handed down within families according to a strict code, which also varies from place to place and family to family. The spells that appear in this book are combinations of stories from the Internet and things I simply made up.

ACKNOWLEDGMENTS

Thank you to my husband and "kids," John, Colin, and Natalie Theys, for being willing readers of outlines and drafts. Special thanks to Colin Theys for valuable insights and suggestions based on his filmmaking expertise, and to Natalie Theys for sharing and encouraging my interest in all things Italian and for being a thought-provoking roomie on our Italian adventures.

A big thank-you to Carmen Johnson, senior editor at Amazon Little A, for seeming to know I wanted to write this even before I did and for giving me the chance to do it. She has been a pleasure to work with and helped make this better at every step of the way. And many thanks to the people who, with sensitivity and thoughtfulness, created and guided the vision for the Kindle in Motion edition: content producers Kjersti Egerdahl and Margaret McCall, art director Tyler Freidenrich, and artists Rebecca Mock and Kouzou Sakai.

Mille grazie to Aila and Alfredo, whose B&B Laguna dei Fenici introduced me to this magical region in Sicily. I hatched the plan for *Children of the Salt Road* in the warm sunshine of their perfect seaside terrace. There was no boy, but there was a frequent mysterious visitor—an exuberant cream-colored puppy.

Finally, thank you to Francis Ford Coppola for hosting Zoetrope, the amazing virtual studio for writers. And to my valued friends there who, over the past fifteen years, have reviewed a story of mine, shared one of their own for me to learn from, offered encouragement, or simply been there to chat with me about life, the universe, and everything—my gratitude.

ABOUT THE AUTHOR

Photo © 2015 Colin Theys

Lydia Fazio Theys writes all the time—technical and marketing writing for a living, fiction because she wants to, and letters of complaint because someone has to. Trained as a scientist, she crossed over to the wordy side pretty early on and has since happily remained. Her creative writing encompasses screenplays, short stories, flash fiction, humor, and narrative nonfiction. Her work has appeared in a variety of online and print publications, been read on public radio, and been used as inspiration by a professional dance theater. Theys currently lives in Woodbridge, Connecticut, where she is at work on her next novel.

Made in the USA
Middletown, DE
26 September 2017